ALSO BY RICHARD PAUL EVANS

Grace
The Gift
Finding Noel
A Perfect Day
The Last Promise
The Christmas Box Miracle
The Carousel
The Looking Glass
The Locket
The Letter
Timepiece
The Christmas Box

For Children
The Dance
The Christmas Candle
The Spyglass
The Tower
The Light of Christmas

✴RICHARD PAUL EVANS✴

THE CHRISTMAS

List

**Doubleday Large Print
Home Library Edition**

SIMON & SCHUSTER
NEW YORK LONDON TORONTO SYDNEY

This Large Print Edition, prepared especially for Doubleday Large Print Home Library, contains the complete, unabridged text of the original Publisher's Edition.

Simon & Schuster
1230 Avenue of the Americas
New York, NY 10020

Copyright © 2009 by Richard Paul Evans

All rights reserved, including the right to reproduce this book or portions thereof in any form whatsoever. For information address Simon & Schuster Subsidiary Rights Department, 1230 Avenue of the Americas, New York, NY 10020

SIMON & SCHUSTER and colophon are registered trademarks of Simon & Schuster, Inc.

ISBN 978-1-61523-497-4

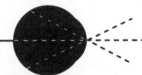

This Large Print Book carries the Seal of Approval of N.A.V.H.

✦ ACKNOWLEDGMENTS ✦

After penning more than a dozen books I'm afraid that my thank you list has become a bit redundant, but my feelings of gratitude have not. I am most appreciative of these people who I have had the pleasure and honor of associating with:
Laurie Liss, Sydny Miner, David Rosenthal, Carolyn Reidy, Gypsy da Silva, Fred Chase

My personal and Christmas Box House team

Lisa V. Johnson, Barry James Evans, Miche Nicole Barbosa, Diane Elizabeth Glad, Heather McVey, Judy Schiffman, Karen Christoffersen, Karen Roylance, Lisa McDonald, Sherri Engar, Doug Smith, and Barbara Thompson.

The Christmas Box International Board

Pat Berckman, Estelle Dahlkemper, Judy Schiffman, Ken Deyhle, Patrice Archibald, Randi Escobar, Kay Dea, Shelly Tripp, Sterling Tanner, Les Moore, Ann Foxley, Lee Farmer, Jean Nielsen, and Mike Olsen.

Special Friends

Glenn Beck, Kevin Balfe, David Parker, Christopher Pair

And, not least, The home team

Keri, Jenna and David Welch, Allyson-Danica, Abigail Hope, McKenna Denece, Richard Michael, and our bulgy-eyed dog: Bello

I am very proud of (and grateful for) my new writing assistant, my daughter, Jenna Evans Welch. Well done, girl. Thank you for your insight. You make me proud.

My love and appreciation to all of you.

✶ To my friend, Robert C. Gay ✶

Dear Reader,

When I was in seventh grade my English teacher, Mrs. Johnson, gave our class the intriguing (if somewhat macabre) assignment of writing our own obituaries. Oddly, I don't remember much of what I wrote about my life, but I do remember how I died: in first place on the final lap of the Daytona 500. At the time I hadn't considered writing as an occupation, a field with a remarkably low on-the-job casualty rate.

What intrigues me most about Mrs. Johnson's assignment is the opportunity she gave us to confront our own legacy.

How do we want to be remembered? That question has motivated our species since the beginning of time: from building pyramids to putting our names on skyscrapers.

As I began to write this book I had two objectives: First, I wanted to explore what could happen if someone read their obituary before they died and saw, firsthand, what the world really thinks of them. Their legacy.

Second, I wanted to write a Christmas story of true redemption. One of my family's holiday traditions is to see a local production of Charles Dickens's *A Christmas Carol.* I don't know how many times I've seen it (perhaps a dozen) but it still thrills me to see the change that comes over Ebenezer Scrooge as he transforms from a dull, tight-fisted miser into a penitent, "giddy-as-a-schoolboy" man with love in his heart. I always leave the show with a smile on my face and a resolve to be a better person. That's what I wanted to share with you, my dear readers, this Christmas—a holiday tale to warm your seasons, your homes, and your hearts.

Merry Christmas,
Richard

THE CHRISTMAS

List

Memo

To: James Kier
From: Linda Nash
Re: The list you requested

Here is the list you requested; the names are in no particular order. Attached is a paragraph about each individual and their relationship to you. I wish you well in your quest, and hope you accomplish what you desire.

Celeste Hatt
Eddie Grimes
Estelle and Karl Wyss
David Carnes
Gary Rossi

P.S. Merry Christmas.

CHAPTER

One

SATURDAY, THREE WEEKS BEFORE CHRISTMAS

James Kier looked back and forth between the newspaper headline and the photograph of himself, not sure if he should laugh or call his attorney. It was the same photograph the *Tribune* had used a couple of years earlier when they featured him on the front page of the business section. He had worn a silver herringbone-weave Armani over a black silk T-shirt for the photo session, the corner of an ebony silk handkerchief peeked strategically from the breast pocket. The black and white photograph was carefully posed and lighted to leave half his face in shadow. The photographer, a black-clad young Japanese man with a shock of bright pink hair, chose to shoot in black and white because, in the photographer's words, he was "going for a yin-yang effect—to fully capture Kier's inner complexities." The photographer was good at his craft. Kier's expression revealed a leaky confidence.

While the photograph was the same, the headline could not have been more different. Not many people get to read their own obituary.

Local real estate mogul dies in automobile crash

Utah real estate developer James Kier was pronounced dead after his car collided with a concrete pylon on southbound I-80. Rescue workers labored for more than an hour to remove the Salt Lake man's body from the wreckage. Authorities believe Kier may have had a heart attack prior to swerving off the road.

Kier was the president of Kier Company, one of the West's largest real estate development firms. He was known as a fierce, oftentimes ruthless, business-man. He once said, "If you want to make friends, join a book club. If you want to make money, go into business. Only a fool confuses the two."

Kier is survived by his son, James Kier II, and his wife, Sara. See page 1 of the business section for more on James Kier.

Kier put the paper down. *Some idiot's going to lose his job over this,* he thought.

He had no idea what the article was about to set in motion.

CHAPTER

Two

Celeste Hatt

Single mother, 29 years old. Son, Henry, 7. Ms. Hatt lost her home after you persuaded her to purchase a larger home than she could afford by putting her entire life's savings into the down payment. Six months later you sold her home at a sizable profit after foreclosing on it. Ms. Hatt's current whereabouts unknown.

ONE DAY EARLIER

Celeste Hatt rooted through a box of children's books looking for the thinnest in the stack. It was definitely a short story night. Barely nine o'clock, and she was already exhausted. The single mother routine never seemed to get easier. During the day, when her son, Henry, was at school, she worked as a checker at Smith's Food and Drug. Weekend evenings she waited tables at the Blue Plate Grill, a small diner half a mile from her home. In addition to her two jobs, nearly every night she assembled circuit boards at home for a local electronics firm. Her tiny kitchen was stacked to the ceiling with brown cardboard boxes printed with Chinese characters.

On most nights, after dinner, the dishes, and her son's homework, she and Henry would watch TV while she snapped the circuit board components together. The process wasn't so much technical as it was tedious; something a machine would be better suited to doing. All the same, it was extra money. Two dollars and fifty cents a board times five an hour equaled thirty dollars a night.

Between her jobs, household chores, and raising an active seven-year-old boy, the only time Celeste had for herself were the few minutes between when Henry went to bed and when her own head hit the pillow. It's been said that the best way to extend the day is to steal a few hours from the night, but there's a price to pay for all theft and it showed in Celeste's dark-ringed eyes. She settled on a book from the pile and carried it into Henry's tiny bedroom. Henry was already in bed, the room illuminated by a small lamp on the floor.

"Hey buddy," she said. "How about *The Grinch*? It's getting near Christmas."

"Okay," he said, leaning up on one el-bow.

She sat down on the side of the bed and opened the book.

Henry brushed a wayward strand of silky blond hair from his face. "Mom, how long are we going to have to live here?"

She looked up from the book. "I don't know, honey. A while."

"How long's a *while*?"

"I wish I knew."

"I don't like it here. I want to go back to *our* house."

Celeste had scrimped, sacrificed, and saved for three years to get them into a home of their own, only to lose it, and their down payment, just five months later. Now they were living in a run-down two-bedroom duplex looking out on the busy thorough-fare of 7th East. It was obvious to her now that she never should have bought the house. *Why had she listened to that man at the development?* Maybe the better ques-tion was, why wouldn't she? He spoke so well, so wisely, like a father giving paternal advice to his daughter. He used logic that seemed irrefutable and words that carried their own persuasive power, like: *home ownership, personal equity, tax deductions,* and *financial security*; each word finding ground in her scared places. She had trusted him to do what was best for her.

"Well, we can't. It's not our house any-more."

"How come?"

"When you don't pay the mortgage the bank takes your house from you."

"What's a mortgage?"

"It's money we borrowed from the bank."

"Why don't you just get more money?"

Celeste sighed. "It's not that easy, sweet-heart."

As she lifted the book again Henry asked, "How come Daddy didn't have to move?"

She frowned. "Do you want a story or not?"

"Okay."

She started to read, fighting to bury the anger Henry's last question brought up. While she battled to keep their heads above water, her ex-husband, Randy, continued to fight her on paying alimony and child support. To make matters worse Henry was struggling in school and his teachers had suggested he needed counseling.

Of course he was struggling. His father had virtually abandoned him, missing the last six months of visits. She wondered how Randy could so easily dismiss this wonderful little boy from his life. The first time her ex didn't show up for his visit, Henry had stood by the door with his suitcase packed for nearly an hour. When Celeste finally got him on the phone he first told her that something had come up but eventually admitted that he had just forgotten and made other plans. He told her that Henry "cramped his style." When she asked if by "style" he meant "selfishness" or "stupidity" he hung up on her.

Henry interrupted again.

"Mom, how is Santa going to find us this year?"

"He'll find us. But don't expect too much. Times are hard for Santa too."

"I'm just going to ask him to make the bank give our house back."

"That would fall under the 'too much' category."

"Not for Santa. He's magic."

Celeste sighed. "Henry, we need to talk about Santa."

He stiffened. "What?"

She looked into his frightened eyes. "Never mind. You know, I'm pretty tired. How about we skip the rest of the story tonight. Okay?"

"All right."

She closed the book and got up off the bed. Henry grabbed her hand. Celeste looked down at him.

"Mom, were you going to tell me there really isn't a Santa?"

"Why would you think that?"

"I already knew. Miss Covey told me."

Celeste felt a prickle of annoyance. "She did, huh?"

He nodded.

"I'm sorry, sweetheart. You should have heard it from me."

"Miss Covey said our parents were lying to us."

Celeste groaned. "Well, I guess I'll be having a talk with Miss Covey."

"*Did* you lie?"

"Henry, Santa is the spirit of giving. And sometimes it's good to have something to believe in. I just wanted you to have something to believe in right now."

"What do *you* believe in?"

She looked at him for a moment then forced a smile. "I believe in you." She combed her fingers through his hair. "And I believe we'll be okay. Now let's say our prayers."

She knelt by the side of his bed. "Would you pray tonight?"

"Sure." Henry closed his eyes. "Dear God . . ." He stopped. Opening one eye he whispered, "Mom?"

"Yes?"

"Is God fake, like Santa Claus?"

"No."

He closed his eyes again. "Heavenly Father. Thank you for our many blessings. Please help Mom to feel better. Help us to get more money. And please help us get our house back. Amen."

"Amen," Celeste said softly. She leaned over and kissed him on the forehead. "I love you, sweetheart."

"I love you too."

She turned off the light, shut the door, then went out into the kitchen. She wished she really believed what she had told her son; that things would be okay. She wished something would happen to make her believe.

Through the kitchen window she could see the snow falling outside. She turned on the radio. "Santa Claus Is Comin' to Town" was playing. Mitch Miller. She turned him off. It was far too festive for how she felt. Thanksgiving had just passed and she and Henry had spent it eating TV dinners with sliced turkey and processed mashed potatoes, then she went into work at the diner. When would something good happen to her?

She heated some water in the microwave, then dropped in a bag of chamomile tea, followed by a teaspoon of honey. She walked to the rocking chair in their front room, stirring her tea, and sat down. A steady flow of cars rolled loudly by. It was like living next to a river that squealed and honked. She took a sip of the tea, then lay her head in her hands and began to cry.

CHAPTER

Three

THAT SAME FRIDAY

Sara's son quietly opened the door and peeked into the darkened room to see if she was still sleeping. Her voice came from the darkness, weak and labored.

"Jimmy?"

"Yes, Mom."

"Is it time?"

"Yes. Almost."

Jimmy's full name was James Kier II, which had a peculiar high ring for the grandson of a humble homebuilder. His name began evolving from the moment he was born, from little Jimmy, to Jim, to J.J., to Jim Jr., finally settling around high school on Jimmy. Jimmy stepped inside the room. "Did I wake you?"

"No, I was just lying here. Would you turn on the light?"

"Sure." Jimmy flipped the light switch. His mother was in her flannel nightgown, the duvet pulled up to her chest, her bald head exposed. Bello, a black shih tzu, nestled in the crevice between her ankles. The dog looked up, then rolled onto his back, hoping to have his belly scratched. "Not now Bello." Sara fumbled around for her cap, found it, and quickly slipped it on. "Sorry," she said, embarrassed. "You shouldn't have to see your mother bald."

Jimmy sat down on the bed next to her. "Some women look pretty bald. You're one of them."

She smiled. "Thank you. Some men look handsome bald."

"And the rest look like thumbs."

Sara laughed. "Are you ready?"

"Yeah. Juliet will be here in a few minutes. At least she had better be or I'll miss my flight."

"I know a couple of girls who wouldn't complain if you did."

"I know a few professors who would."

"I know. Here, give me a love."

She pulled him in close and held him as tightly as she could. "It's been so nice having you home. I miss you when you're gone."

"I miss you too, Mom." He reached over and stroked the dog's long silky fur. "How's Bells?"

"He's a pain," she said. "Can't live with him. Can't grill him."

Jimmy laughed, then slid his fingers under Bello's collar and scratched his neck. "And how are you feeling?"

"I'm okay," she said.

He looked up at her dubiously. "Yeah?"

"Maybe a little dizzy."

"You should go back to sleep."

"I need to get up. I have a meeting this morning."

Jimmy's brow furrowed. "What kind of meeting?"

She hesitated, knowing her answer would make him angry. "With your father and the lawyers."

Jimmy reacted as she expected. "You've got to be kidding!"

"It's okay."

"What's okay? That he drags you out of

bed at his convenience? The heck with him. You just had chemo."

"I agreed to the meeting. It was today or next week." Sara exhaled. "I need to get this over with."

"I don't know why you bother with him. He's a cold-blooded, selfish . . ."

"Jimmy. Stop." Sara spoke more sharply than she meant to.

"You know he is."

"Don't talk about him that way. He's your father."

"No jury would convict him of that." He looked at his mother and felt bad for upsetting her. "I'm sorry. But for your sake, not his."

She put her hand on his. "I understand your anger, Jimmy, but I don't like it. If I don't make it through this, he'll be the only parent you have."

"Mom, don't talk that way. You're going to beat this."

"Of course I will. I just want you to think about it."

He exhaled in exasperation. "I just don't get it, Mom. Why are you still so loyal to him? He left you when you needed him the most."

Sara looked at her son sadly. "History, I suppose. I know why your father is the way he is. And I believe there's still a good man inside of him. He's just lost himself for a while."

"How do you know he's not lost forever?"

"We all get lost sometimes. The trick is to believe that we're worth finding."

Jimmy smiled ruefully. "All right. Do you need a ride?"

"I'll be fine. And *you* have a plane to catch." She gently rubbed his hand. "How are the wedding plans coming?"

"Fine, I guess. Juliet and her mom have had trouble finding a reception center open on New Year's Day. Everything available is too expensive."

"I wish they would let us help."

"I know. But her parents won't hear of it. Anyway, Juliet is pretty much taking care of everything. She's run me ragged the few days I've been here. The tuxedo shop, bridal photos, caterers. I can't wait for vacation to be over so I can get some rest."

Sara smiled. "Juliet's a sweet girl. And it's a special day for her, marrying the perfect man. You only get one of those." She squeezed her son's hand. "When do you get back?"

"My last final is on the nineteenth. I leave that afternoon."

"We'll be waiting."

Just then a car honked. "There's Jules. I'll have her come in."

"No, you better run. You don't want to miss your flight. And Juliet's going to want every second with you she can have."

Jimmy smiled and stood but hesitated. He sensed that his mother wasn't telling him everything. "Mom?"

"Yes, darling?"

"I'm worried about leaving you. I don't feel like it's the right thing."

"Nonsense. I'm doing fine. And I have plenty of help and the best of care. Just go finish school and come back. I'm not going anywhere."

He looked at her a moment then forced a smile. "You better not be."

"I promise." Sara's eyes filled with tears. "'Bye sweetheart. Good luck on your finals."

"'Bye, Mom." Jimmy leaned over and kissed her on the forehead, then walked out of the room. Sara waited until she heard the front door close, then swung her legs over the side of the bed, and, clutching the bedpost for support, got to her feet. She had less strength than she let on to those around her. She could feel herself growing weaker each day like a clock running down.

As she walked slowly to the shower she thought about the upcoming wedding. She wished that she could be more involved with the preparations but she didn't have the energy. The truth was she knew there was a possibility that she wouldn't even be around long enough to see it. Though Jimmy still clung to the hope that she would recover, it was only because he didn't know how sick she really was. Only Sara and her doctor knew just how far her cancer had progressed and Sara wasn't willing to lay that burden on her child. She never told him that the treatments she was undergoing weren't meant to cure her—they were meant to manage her pain and prolong her life. If she could buy enough time she would realize her final goal of seeing her only child married. Then she was done, she told herself, and it didn't matter what happened to her. At least that's what she told herself.

CHAPTER

Four

Juliet climbed out of the car just as Jimmy emerged from the house, wheeling his suitcase behind him. "Good morning, handsome!"

Jimmy smiled as she ran up to him. His fiancée wore a white wool coat and her short blond hair was mostly hidden beneath a bright red wool cap. "Hey, babe."

She met him halfway down the walk. They embraced, then kissed.

"This is killing me," Juliet said. "I can't believe I have to say goodbye again."

"Last time," Jimmy said. "Then you won't be able to get rid of me."

She looked into his eyes. "Promise?"

"Promise." Jimmy kissed her again. "We'd better hurry." He threw his suitcase in the back of her car. "Want me to drive?"

"Yes, sir."

Jimmy opened the door for her, then walked around the car and climbed behind the wheel.

"I'm sorry I'm late," she said. "My dad's car wouldn't start and he was parked behind me."

"We'll get there in time. What's wrong with his car?"

"Battery or altersomething. It's old."

They backed out of the driveway. At the first corner Juliet asked, "How's your mom this morning?"

Jimmy shook his head. "That depends on if you go by what she says or how she looks. As far as I can tell, she's not getting any better."

"Chemo's hard. It will take time. But she's a strong woman."

"That she is."

"I'll check up on her while you're gone. I was thinking of asking her out to lunch this week."

"She'd love that."

Juliet's face lit up. "Oh, I've got great news. Mom and I found a place."

Jimmy looked at her quizzically. "A place for what?"

"Wow, that is *so* revealing. A place for our wedding, dummy."

"That's great, Jules. Where?"

"It's this adorable reception center. It's a bit more expensive than we hoped, but my mom asked if they could come down a little on the price, and they said being New Year's Day they might be able to do something. I can't believe it's available. It's the most beautiful place we looked at. It's just perfect."

Jimmy was happy to see her so excited. "That's a relief. Tell me about it."

"It's in Sandy and has the most amazing view of the mountains. It's kind of like a greenhouse, so it has fountains and plants everywhere like a labyrinth, you can kind of get lost in it. I think it used to be a flower shop."

Jimmy's brow furrowed. "It's not Le Jardin, is it?"

"You know the place?"

"It won't work."

Juliet's smile fell. "What do you mean it won't work? It's perfect. And it's available."

"My father owns it."

She looked at him quizzically. "Isn't that even better?"

"No."

"Jimmy, I don't understand."

"To begin with, it would mean we'd have to invite him."

Juliet was even more confused. "You're not inviting your father to our wedding?"

"No. I don't want him there. You'll have to find someplace else."

"Just like that?" she said.

"Le Jardin is not an option."

"Mom and I have spent *weeks* looking for a place. It's the only option."

"No it's not. We can do what I originally suggested and rent the ballroom at the Grand America."

"And where do we find the money for that?"

"We'll pay for it."

She turned away from him. "I'm not going to have this conversation again."

"I think we should."

"Do you have any idea how embarrassing this is for my parents? It's easy for you to just throw money around; my parents have saved for years for this day."

"All the more reason my family should pay for it."

"You don't understand."

"You're right, I don't. Your parents are being . . ." He stopped himself.

"My parents are being what? Stupid?"

"Proud."

"They should be proud. They've worked hard to give me everything they could. You can't just take that away from them."

"That's not what I meant to do."

"It doesn't matter what you *meant* to do, it's what you're *doing*. You have no idea what it's like to not have money." Juliet leaned against the door, crying.

As they entered the Salt Lake airport, Jimmy exhaled. "Jules, I'm sorry." He reached over and touched her thigh. "I'm really sorry." Without looking she took his hand. He drove up to the first terminal and pulled up between two cars to the curb.

He leaned over. "Come on, let's not leave each other this way."

Juliet wiped her eyes. "Okay." She leaned her head on his shoulder. "It's not just the reception. I know your father wasn't there for you, but leaving him out of the wedding is wrong. I'm afraid that someday you'll regret it."

Jimmy held her close, but didn't answer. "I just want you to be happy."

"I promise I'll think about it," he said. They kissed. "We *could* always elope."

"I couldn't do that to my family. My sisters are so excited to be bridesmaids. And I'm excited to be your bride. You should see my dress. It's gorgeous."

"Like you."

They kissed again. Just then an airport police officer rapped on the door. "People, this is an active zone," she said.

"Sorry," Jimmy said. He popped the trunk and they both climbed out. They kissed one more time on the curb. Juliet's eyes glistened with tears. "Come home soon, I love you."

"I love you too. More than I ever believed possible." Jimmy grabbed his bag and walked inside. He waved one more time before entering the terminal. Juliet blew him a kiss. The police officer walked up to her.

"Husband?"

"Almost," she said.

"Best kind," the woman said. "Now let's save you a ticket and get this car out of here."

CHAPTER

Five

The Friday the newspaper reported James Kier's death began just like any other. At six A.M. Kier met Tim Brey, his company's chief operating officer, for their weekly game of squash. As usual, Kier won every set. Afterward he stopped at the 4th South Starbucks where he drank a Venti latte while he read the day's headlines from the *Salt Lake Tribune*, the *Wall Street Journal* and the *Financial Times*, then he drove home, showered and dressed. Although he was usually at work by nine, today he had a meeting with a jeweler. He was designing a ring for his girlfriend's Christmas present: a two-karat marquis-cut diamond set in a wide platinum band.

Even though there was a private entry in the rear of the building, Kier always entered through the front door so his employees would know he was there. It was not without effect. At his arrival employees stopped their idle chatter and sprang to work as quickly as motorists hitting their brakes at the first sight of a highway patrolman.

(A reporter once asked Kier how many people worked at Kier Company. He replied, "About half of them.")

He passed the front desk and walked down the corridor to where his secretary, Linda Nash, sat at the entrance to his corner office.

The Kier building was plain by design—a work space built for function not frills. "A picture on the wall doesn't make me money," Kier was fond of saying. What decor existed—a few plants and wall hangings— had been put there years earlier by his wife, Sara. Even though it was past Thanksgiving, the office was conspicuously devoid of holiday dressing. Kier didn't believe in wasting money on seasonal frivolities and made it a point to belittle those who did.

As he approached his office, Linda looked up from her computer. "Good morning, Mr. Kier." She was in her late thirties, slender with long, dishwater blond hair that she wore pulled back in a low ponytail.

"Is the meeting still on?"

"Everyone's waiting for you in the conference room."

Kier took off his coat and laid it on Linda's desk. "My ex-wife and her lawyer are in the conference room and you call it a 'good' morning?"

"I'm sorry, Mr. Kier." She hung his coat on a coat rack near his office door.

"When's my next meeting?"

"At ten o'clock. Mr. Vance Allen with Scott Homes."

"Allen," he repeated. "Well, don't talk to him. I want him on edge. And get me my coffee."

"Would you like it in the conference room?"

"No, I don't expect to be in there that long."

He turned and walked away.

"Yes sir," she said softly.

Kier walked down the hall to his conference room. The long polished table of bird's-eye maple could seat twelve, but that morning it had only three occupants: two lawyers and his wife. Kier's lawyer, Lincoln Archibald, was a barrel-chested man with a full head of thick black hair that spilled over into bushy Elvis-style sideburns. His sideburns had once been even longer, until Kier, not one to hide his opinions, asked Lincoln if he wore the things on a bet or if he was trying to frighten children. The next time Kier saw him the sideburns had been trimmed.

Sara had her back to the entry, as did her lawyer, Steve Pair, who was Sara's nephew and fresh from law school. Kier wasn't fond of Sara's sister, Beth, and held her son in the same low regard.

Kier slumped down in the seat next to Lincoln, quietly groaning to let everyone know what an annoyance he considered the meeting. Only then did he look at his wife. Sara wore a silk scarf around her head beneath a red, sharp-rimmed cloche. Even though they'd been separated for nearly a year she still wore the simple, quarter-karat ring with which he'd wed her on her left hand. She was always well put together, and even though she looked pale her lash-less eyes were still piercing. Kier turned away from her gaze. He felt—had always felt—that she could look right through him.

"Sara," he said shortly, nodding.

"Hello, Jim."

"You don't look so well."

"I'm fine." It was obvious that she wasn't. She was sickly pale and had obviously lost weight since the last time Kier had seen her, three weeks earlier. "We missed you on Thanksgiving."

"I was out of town. It was a last-minute thing."

"Jimmy was here. You could have met his fiancée."

"Like I said, I was out of town."

"Shall we get started?" Steve asked.

Kier turned and faced the young lawyer. "What do you call a criminal lawyer?" Kier asked.

"Excuse me?"

"I said, what do you call a criminal law-yer?"

Steve looked at Kier with annoyance. "I don't know. What do you call a criminal lawyer?"

"A redundancy."

Steve just shook his head. "Okay, with that out of the way, we'll begin. Against my counsel, my client, Mrs. Kier, has generously agreed to accept all of your terms, except for two. She would like to keep the piano. It has sentimental value. Also, there's not enough money for Jimmy's education."

Kier's grin vanished. "Jimmy can work his way through school like I did. And what does he need college for anyway? He just wants to paint his little pictures."

"Mr. Kier, we both know my client—"

"Your *client*? Are you stupid? She's your aunt. Her name is Sara."

Sara looked apologetically at Steve, then back at Kier. "Please, Jim, let's keep this civil."

Kier settled back, crossing his arms and glancing down at his watch. "Fine. Let's get this over with."

Steve started again. "I have advised my . . . Sara to either get the money for Jimmy's education or we're going back for business assets."

Kier glared at the young man. Lincoln leaned over and whispered into his ear. "Take it."

The truth was Kier neither wanted the

piano nor really cared about the price of Jimmy's tuition. He was a negotiator and the first rule of any negotiation is to ask for things you don't care about in case you need to bargain for something of real value.

He exhaled loudly. "All right. It's his life. Why should I care how he wastes it?"

Steve glanced at Sara, then turned back to Lincoln. "Very well, then there's nothing more to discuss. I'll have the new language added to the agreement and the documents over to you by Monday."

Kier stood. "Just get it over with. I want this mistake behind me."

Sara looked down, trying to hide her hurt. Kier felt foolish and tried to diffuse the awkwardness. "So, Steve-o. What do you call a thousand lawyers at the bottom of the ocean."

"A good start," Steve said tersely, collecting papers and putting them into his attaché case.

"You learn that in law school?"

"Among other things."

"At least it wasn't a total waste," Kier said beneath his breath.

Sara stood and walked over to Kier. She held out her hand. "Goodbye, Jim." Kier felt embarrassed for his comment. "I didn't mean that."

"Oh?" she said, "Then what did you mean?"

Kier looked at her blankly, at a loss for words.

Suddenly Sara fell backward. Kier lunged to grab her but Steve caught her from behind.

"Here," Kier said, pushing a chair forward. "Sit her down."

Steve helped her into the chair.

"I'm sorry," Sara said. "I'm just a little weak."

"Are you going to be all right?" Kier asked.

She looked up at him. "I'm not your problem anymore."

Kier turned away. "I've got a meeting." He walked out the door and back to his office.

✳

Linda looked up as he approached. "That was quick."

"It was an eternity. Where's Allen?"

"Mr. Allen isn't here yet. I put his file on your desk next to your coffee. And Miss Steele called. Shall I get her on the phone?"

"Yes. And Sara's not feeling well. Get

her a Coke or something." He walked into his office and shut the door behind him.

✳

Kier's phone buzzed as he sank into his chair. He pushed the speaker button. "Hey baby, what's up?"

A deep voice answered, "It's me, baby. Lincoln."

"Where are you?"

"I'm walking to my car. Look, I say we don't sign the papers."

"We just got everything we wanted."

"Yes, but you're still giving up the house, your IRAs, and the Waterford investment account. I say we just put this on ice."

"Why the sudden change of heart?"

"I hadn't seen Sara for a while. If we hold off long enough, as the surviving partner you'll end up with everything."

"You're a hard man, Lincoln."

"From you, I'll take that as a compliment."

Linda beeped in. "Miss Steele's on the line."

"I've got to go."

"You know I'm right," Lincoln said.

"You're a heartless mercenary."

"That's why you hired me. Let me know."

"'Bye." He pushed another button. "Hey baby."

"Hi big guy. Guess what I'm wearing?"

"I have no idea."

"Close your eyes."

"And?"

"Are they closed?"

"Yes," he lied.

"Okay, now imagine me in very, *very* tiny pieces of string and fabric some scandalous fashion designer called a bikini. Inch per inch this thing is more expensive than Manhattan real estate. I think we should fly to Boca Raton for the weekend and try it out."

"Boca's too far."

"Did I mention I bought a new bikini?"

"Our trip to Cancún set me back a week at work. I'm still paying for it."

"And wasn't I worth it? All work and no play makes Jimmy a dull boy."

"All play and no work makes Jimmy a *poor* boy."

"It would take a lot of play to do that."

"How about something closer?"

"How close?"

"Something that doesn't require an airport."

"I was prepared for that. Plan B, Park City. I know a quaint little bed-and-breakfast with in-room hot tubs. Can you get off a little early?"

"I could cancel a meeting. What time are you thinking?"

"Around five."

Linda beeped in again. "Mr. Allen is here."

"Five? Okay. I'll cancel my meeting. I've got to go. I'll transfer you to Linda; she can make the reservations."

"If you must."

"What does that mean?"

"I hate talking to her. She's so . . . boring. And I don't think she likes me."

"I didn't hire her because she's entertaining and it doesn't matter if she likes you. I'll see you at lunch."

"Ciao, baby."

＊

With Vance Allen waiting outside his office, Kier walked around his desk and moved the chairs a little further back. He was always mindful of taking the psychological advantage. When he first moved in, he had a carpenter cut nearly two inches off the legs of his guest chairs as well as an additional half inch off the front so the occupant was not only forced to look up to him but always felt a little off balance. On one occasion, when negotiating a multimillion-dollar real estate purchase, he had slipped Dramamine into his client's coffee to make him drowsy. To Kier, all was fair in business.

He went back to his desk and opened the file Linda had left for him on Vance Allen. Five months earlier Allen had come to him in desperate need of nearly a million dollars. ($974,076 to be exact. Kier was always exact.) Vance had been in danger of losing a family-owned, forty-six-acre property near the base of Little Cottonwood Canyon that was in tax arrears. To secure the property Allen had to find money quickly and came to Kier for a hard money loan. It was a prime piece of real estate, easily worth five times the amount of the loan. Kier currently held the deed and would prefer it stayed that way. He pressed the speakerphone button; "Let him in."

Vance stepped in to his office. He was a tall, clumsy-looking man with graying temples. Kier thought him a simpleton who liked to shake hands too much. He made it a point to use hand sanitizer after their meetings.

"Mr. Kier, it's a pleasure to see you."

Kier sat back, his gaze cold. "Have a seat."

Vance sat down, sensing the awkwardness of the chair. He furtively glanced down at the chair's front legs.

"You've got my money?"

Vance looked up and smiled weakly. "Well, okay, right to business. As you know, the loan call date is about three weeks from now, on the twenty-fourth of December. The good news is that I've found an investor. However, he's going to have to liquidate some assets and it's going to take him until the new year to come up with all the capital. So, if it's okay with you, I'd like to extend the loan for an extra few weeks, with points and interest of course."

Kier just looked at him. "No."

Allen's surprise was evident on his face. "No?"

"That wasn't our arrangement and I need my money back. You've had six months to close the deal. We have payment in full by the twenty-fourth or you default and we take the property."

Allen's jaw tightened. "But our investor can't come up with the money that fast. We're only talking an extra three or four weeks."

"That's not my problem. We have a deal and I expect you to live up to it. Honorably."

Allen turned red. "I've never cheated anyone in my entire life."

"Good. Let's keep it that way."

"It's the danged economy, trying to find a jumbo loan right now is almost impossible."

"We're all having hard times. Now, I'm busy. I'll see you with my money on the twenty-fourth."

"This property has been in my family for almost a hundred years."

Kier looked down for a moment, then back at Vance. "Tell you what. When we start building we'll name the development after your great-granddad."

Vance was trembling with anger. Without another word he stood up and walked out of the office. After the door shut, Kier habitually took out his hand sanitizer and

rubbed it into his hands, then started looking through the P&L reports his accoun-
tant had left on his desk.

A few minutes later Linda buzzed him.

"What is it?"

"Your Park City reservations are con-
firmed."

"I need you to cancel my four-thirty
meeting with Dawson."

"I already have. Would you like me to
reschedule?"

"Monday, if I have anything open."

"Anything else, Mr Kier?"

"No."

"It's nice you're getting away."

"Why, glad to be rid of me?" Kier snorted.

"No, sir. I was just thinking it's nice to
get away sometimes."

Kier disconnected and Linda set her
phone down. After her husband Max became ill with multiple sclerosis, traveling
was pretty much out of the question. She
couldn't remember the last time she had
been on a real vacation.

✦

While Kier was meeting with Vance, Steve
walked Sara out to her car, holding her
arm through the parking lot. "Well, we got

what you asked for," Steve said, clearly displeased. When Sara didn't respond he added, "We really should have gone for more. Much more."

"I don't need more."

"You should be looking out for your future."

Sara gave him a wry smile. "Well, there's not much point to that, is there?"

"Aunt Sara, you shouldn't talk that way."

"I'm just being realistic."

Steve opened the car door for her. "Would you like me to drive you home? I can have someone from the office pick up my car."

"I'll be okay." Sara sat down in the car and put the keys in the ignition.

"You know, Aunt Sara, I don't understand how someone like you ends up with a creep like that."

"Jim wasn't always like this."

"The way he treats people is obscene. Especially the way he treats you."

Sara ignored her nephew's comment. "Thank you for your help, Steve. And I still haven't received a bill for your services."

"Nor will you."

"I insist."

"Favorite aunts don't get billed. Unless you happen to be making some of those tiger rolls you always bring to the family Christmas party, then I'll accept payment in kind."

Sara smiled. "I'll make a few extra rolls just for you."

"Consider me in your debt."

"Thank you, Steve. Tell your mother hello for me."

He stepped back from the car and shut the door. "Drive carefully."

As Sara drove away he said to himself, "That idiot is throwing away the best thing he's ever had."

CHAPTER

Six

Kier had met his girlfriend, Traci Steele a year earlier at a real estate showing less than a week after he had separated from Sara. She was nine years younger than he, though she looked even younger. Traci was a stunningly attractive, curvaceous brunette, the quintessential trophy wife.

At noon he picked her up from her condo in Alpine and they drove to a French bistro just outside Orem. The maîtred' sat them at Kier's regular table, in the corner near a large window that overlooked the back garden. The yard was covered in snow and ice glistened from the garden statuary. Traci broke off a piece of croissant and buttered it. "So how was my sweetie's morning?"

"I met with my wife and her attorney."

"Oh, that sounds fun. Did we win?"

"We settled."

"Just settled?"

"We won." He looked down at his menu. "Sara's not looking well. I think she's sicker than she lets on."

"That's too bad. So when is it over?"

"When is what over?"

"The marriage."

"I don't know. Soon. Now Lincoln is recommending that I don't sign anything and just wait."

"Wait for what?"

Kier looked up from his menu. "For Sara to die."

Traci wrinkled her nose. "Oh that's cold, even for a lawyer."

Kier frowned, tired of the conversation. "So what are you having?"

"The Caesar salad with shrimp."

"Tell me about this bed-and-breakfast you booked us in to."

"You make it sound like a jail. I promise you, you'll love it. It's called the Snowed Inn. That's I-n-n."

"Yeah, I get it."

Traci ignored his tone. "It's very quaint. And every room has a hot tub."

"So I'll make dinner reservations for six?"

"Oh . . ."

"Oh?"

"I can't get up there until eight."

"Eight? You said five. I canceled a meeting so I could take off early."

"Oh honey, I know. I'm so sorry. I forgot that Mercedes has a dance recital and I can't miss it. The last time I did she beat me up with it for two months. And then she told her shrink what an awful mom I am."

"A dance recital?"

"Why don't you come with me to the recital and then we'll drive up together?"

"A dance recital? I'd rather chew razor blades. I'll just go up early. I can get a nap in."

"Good. Then you won't be so grumpy when I get there." Traci leaned over and kissed him on the cheek.

"I'm not grumpy."

A waiter appeared and quietly cleared his throat. "Are you ready to order?"

Kier looked up. "I'll have the filet Oscar, she'll have the Caesar salad."

"With shrimp," Traci added.

"Anything to drink?"

"Just a Coke. What do you want?"

"A chardonnay."

"Very well," the waiter said. "I'll be right back with your drinks." He left.

Traci took his hand. "I'm sorry I'm going to be late. I'll make it up to you. We can eat a late dinner, go dancing, then whatever . . . Just don't pout. I hate it when you pout."

"I don't pout."

"Well, whatever it is you're doing." She looked out over the yard. "It's snowing again. It's supposed to snow all weekend. Maybe we'll get snowed in. Wouldn't that be great? Snowed in at the Snowed—"

"Yeah, I get it."

She buttered another piece of croissant. "Do you know why these are so good? They brush them with egg before they bake them. It makes them shiny like that." She took a bite. "I took a French cooking class once. Maybe I'll cook you a meal for our anniversary. Our anniversary *is* coming up."

"Oh?"

"You forgot?"

He smiled. "No. I've got a surprise for you."

She smiled back. "I like surprises. Usually."

"You'll like this one."

"I can't wait."

"You'll have to."

"You're mean. I can see why your wife left you."

"I left her."

"Like I said, you're mean."

CHAPTER

Seven

Kier drove Traci back to her condo, then returned to the office. Tim Brey was waiting for him in the conference room. The table was covered with blue and white building plans.

"There they are," Brey said. "The final plans for the Paradise development."

"Did we get the permits?"

"No, but it's only a formality. We have the final zoning meeting tonight."

"Good thing we own the committee," Kier said. He looked over the plans, nodding approvingly. "I want to modify this for something around forty acres."

Brey looked up. "We're getting the Allen property?"

"Unless he finds a million dollars in the next three weeks."

Brey smiled. "Well done. You said you were going to end up with that piece."

Kier lifted his case. "Set a meeting with the architects. We'll go over it Monday afternoon."

"Done. Let me know how the hearing goes tonight."

Kier stopped. "I forgot about that. You better handle it."

"But . . ." Brey stopped himself.

"Is there a problem?" Kier raised an eyebrow.

Brey had plans with his wife, plans made weeks ago, but he knew better than to mention them. "No problem."

"Good man." Kier patted his shoulder and walked out of the room.

✦

Kier stopped by his office and grabbed his briefcase and a bottle of water. "I'm out of here," he said to Linda.

"Be careful out there. I checked the weather report. Park City is expecting a blizzard. They say that they could get two to three feet of snow tonight."

"When does it hit?"

"Later this afternoon, probably after rush hour. Do you need anything?"

"Call Lincoln, tell him to prepare the paperwork on the Allen property."

"I will. Have a good weekend."

"You too."

Kier walked out the back door to his car. He started his car, then turned on his stereo, which began to play a Michael Bublé CD Traci had given him. He smiled as he considered the Allen property. It was worth a fortune. He drove out of the parking lot and headed for Park City.

CHAPTER

Eight

The storm arrived early as Kier drove his arctic white BMW up the canyon toward Park City, his wipers flipping frantically to keep up with the snowfall. On both sides of him the canyon walls rose jagged and white, plastered with ice and snow. The traffic around him had slowed to a crawl and cars, covered in snow, moved slowly, like a herd of mobile igloos. It bothered him that he couldn't get Sara off his mind. How she looked. Her fall. Her last words to him—*I'm not your problem anymore.* He realized that he had never really confronted the reality of her dying.

Christmas Day would have been their silver anniversary: a quarter of a century. Kier hadn't much experience with death. His mother had died when he was two; he didn't remember her or her passing. His father had died six years ago, but they hadn't spoken for years and he didn't even attend the funeral. But Sara was different. He wondered how long she had left and how her death would affect him.

He took a drink from his bottle of water and set it on the seat next to him. He couldn't figure out why Sara had delayed their divorce for so long. It clearly wasn't about money; she asked for much less than she was entitled to and they both knew it. He was still puzzling over this when he arrived at the Park City junction. In another ten minutes he turned off the highway to the Snowed Inn bed-and-breakfast. Traci would be up in a few hours. He could worry about Sara later.

CHAPTER

Nine

The Snowed Inn was a large Victorian with three great gables set above a wraparound front porch. White Christmas lights outlined the building, creating a thin halo in the pale fog. Broad red ribbon was wrapped around the porch's supporting pillars giving them the appearance of giant peppermint sticks. The two front doors were garnished with pine wreaths adorned with silver and red baubles.

Kier parked his car. When he reached for his cell phone on the seat next to him his hand found a pool of water and his phone in it. He lifted it, dripping. The screen was blank, Kier pushed the buttons on the keypad but nothing happened. He angrily threw it on the car floor. Then he climbed out of the car, grabbed a small sports bag from the trunk, and walked up the steps into the inn.

The Snowed Inn had originally been built at the end of the nineteenth century as a home by Clayton Daly, a successful silver prospector and co-owner of the Daly-West Silver Mine. When Daly was killed in an explosion in the mine, his wife had tried to support her family by turning the home into a boardinghouse. Within a few years World War I lowered the price of silver and as prospectors left the town, the building became just another relic of a ghost town. When developers rediscovered the city in the late sixties the old building was revived as a bed-and-breakfast and had done well ever since.

Just inside the door, under a daguerro-type of Clayton Daly, was a crescent-shaped walnut counter. Behind it stood a portly, silver-haired man wearing a red flannel shirt and brown corduroy pants with blue suspenders. He smiled as Kier entered. "Good afternoon, sir. Welcome to the Snowed Inn."

Kier, still angry about his phone, was in no mood for pleasantries. "I've got a reservation," he said curtly. "It's under Kier."

"Yes, Mr. Kier, we've been expecting you. You have a very pleasant secretary, I might add. Your secretary left a credit card number with me, so if you'll just sign right here I can take you right up to your room."

Kier signed the registry. "Do you have Internet access?"

"We have wireless in every room. The access code is printed on the keycard sleeve. How many keys do you need?"

"Two, but I want to leave one here. My companion won't be here until eight or so."

"Very good," he said, lifting a pen. "Her name?"

"Traci."

He wrote her name on the key sleeve. "Traci. Do you need help with your bag?"

"Of course not. Just call my room when she arrives."

"I'll be sure to do that. You're right around the corner and up the stairs. My name is

Fred if you need anything. We begin serving breakfast at six."

"What time does it end?"

"Eleven. Have a good stay."

✦

Once inside his room, Kier set his bag on an end table, then pulled out his laptop and logged into the hotel's network. He checked over his e-mails and the Dow Jones, then closed his computer and walked over to open the television cabinet. The remote was on top of the television. He lay back on the bed and surfed channels until he came across the University of Utah Utes playing the ASU Sundevils. The game was only halfway through the first quarter; he propped several pillows up behind him and lay back to watch. Before the end of the first quarter he was asleep.

✦

When he awoke, the room was dark except for the glow of the television; a weatherman was talking in excited tones about the blizzard. Kier checked his watch: 10:22. He instinctively reached for his cell phone, then remembered that he no longer had one. He picked up the room phone and called the front desk. "This is James Kier in 211. I was expecting a guest; has she called?"

"No sir, but I'll call you the moment she arrives. The weather has probably delayed her."

"Probably." He hung up and dialed Traci's cell phone but she didn't answer. This didn't surprise him since she made it a point to never answer calls from phone numbers she didn't recognize. It crossed his mind that she could have been stuck in the canyon or worse, but he let it pass. *She got me all the way up here; she better have a good excuse.* He lay back, angry. Within a few minutes he fell asleep again.

CHAPTER

Ten

The sun broke through the east windows, waking Kier to a clear, bright morning. He was still in his clothes and still alone. He looked at his watch and groaned. It was past nine. He rolled over to the phone and called the desk.

"This is Jim Kier in 211. Was the canyon closed last night?"

"I don't believe so. We had guests arrive past midnight."

"Did anyone leave a message for me?"

"Just a minute." The man was gone just a few seconds. "Sorry, sir, I have no messages. But we do have breakfast ready. This morning we're serving our cheese and sausage omelet, homemade granola, fresh squeezed orange juice, buckwheat pan—"

"All right. I'll be down."

Kier hung up. From outside he could hear the scraping blade of a snowplow. He walked over to the window; it had stopped snowing but it looked like the storm had dumped over a foot of snow. In the parking lot below a red Ford pickup with a plow was clearing the parking lot, pushing snow into banks taller than the truck itself. It occurred to him why she hadn't called. *She probably tried my cell,* he thought. Kier changed into his sweats and went downstairs. There were several couples already in the dining room. Fred greeted him with a pot of coffee.

"Good morning, Mr. Kier. Would you care for some coffee?"

"I'd like some decaf."

"Right away. I have a nice little brew called the Mormon Blend."

Fred walked back to the kitchen. When he returned a few minutes later he was holding a coffeepot in one hand and a folded newspaper in the other. As he poured the coffee he said, "I want to show you something I think you'll find interesting." He laid the newspaper out on the table. "You not only have the same name as this fellow, but you look an awful lot alike."

Kier took a sip of coffee as he cast an uninterested glance at the paper. "I look nothing like John McCain."

"No, sir, the article below that."

Kier scanned the page until he saw the picture. Above it was the headline:

Local real estate mogul dies in automobile crash

Kier set down his coffee. "What the . . ."

Utah real estate developer James Kier was pronounced dead after his car collided with a concrete pylon on southbound I-80. Rescue workers labored for more than an hour to remove the Salt Lake man's body from the wreckage. Authorities believe Kier may have had a heart attack prior to swerving off the road.

Kier was the president of Kier Company, one of the West's largest real estate development firms. He was known as a fierce, oftentimes ruthless, businessman. He once said, "If you want to make friends, join a book club. If you want to make money, go into business. Only a fool confuses the two."

Kier is survived by his son, James Kier II and his wife, Sara. See page 1 of the business section for more on James Kier.

Kier stared at the picture. "That's me," he said. He set down his coffee, "This is . . . crazy."

"Maybe that's why your guest didn't come."

"You might be right." He reflexively reached for his cell phone and again remembered he no longer had one. "Never mind breakfast, I've got to make some calls."

"Here, take a pastry with you." Fred quickly retrieved a cheese Danish from the buffet table and wrapped it in a napkin. "Wife made 'em."

"Thank you." Kier took the pastry and his coffee and returned to his room. His first call was to Traci. Still no answer and her voice mailbox was full. *Not surprising*, he thought, *she must be inundated with calls about me.*

Next he called Lincoln, who answered on the first ring.

"Hello."

"What's the difference between a lawyer and a vulture?"

There was silence on the other end of the line.

"The lawyer gets frequent flier miles."

"Who is this?"

"Who do you think, monkey boy?

There was another long pause. "Kier?"

"Back from the dead."

Lincoln started to laugh. "It's really you. I've been freaking out here. I thought you were dead. Or do they have pay phones in hell?"

"No, they have cell phones, they just drop the call every five seconds."

Lincoln laughed again. "Where are you calling from?"

"Park City."

"This is surreal. When Carol called to tell me, I didn't believe her. But when I tried to call you, there was no answer."

"Well, my cell phone *did* die."

"So what happened?"

"I don't know yet. I'm guessing that the reporter got the wrong Kier. By the way, I want you to sue him and the rag he writes for. I want to own the thing."

"I'll start checking for precedents. Of course we'll have to show damage, but that shouldn't be too hard. You know, there's more than just the local paper. There's been television and radio coverage not to mention the Net. There's a whole river of comments up on the paper's Web site already."

"Really?" Kier said. "That should be interesting."

"I don't recommend you read them."

"And why is that?"

"You know how people are. The Internet is the bathroom stall of media."

"What, no respect for the dead?" Kier said sarcastically.

"Not exactly."

"Whatever. I'm headed back to town. Assuming the roads are clear, I'll be home in a couple of hours. I need to get a new phone."

"Talk to you later, chief. And congratulations."

"For what?"

"Not being dead."

✦

Kier hung up the phone, showered and shaved. As he was getting dressed his curiosity got the better of him and he went to the Web site of the *Salt Lake Tribune*. His story was third down on the local page. Underneath the story was a stream of comments.

Maguire17: Ding dong the wicked Kier is dead!!!!

LFB09: Someone must have thrown a bucket of water on him.

Mojo777: The article said Kier died of a heart attack before he crashed his car. I thought you had to have a heart to have a heart attack.

LFB09: Kier had a bank vault where his heart should have been.

Mojo777: Fitting that the car burst into flames. Just getting him used to where he's going.

Hope17: Show some respect for the dead.

Mojo777: Why should we? Kier showed no respect for the living.

Supertramp11: Amen to that. He was divorcing his wife while she had cancer. They served her the same day she got home from her first chemo treatment. Who does that?

Mojo777: Apparently he really had it out for cancer sufferers. Didn't you read the story about his evicting that man dying of cancer?

Prowler2000: Kier should have died of cancer. Slow, painful cancer. Would have been poetic.

Maguire17: My neighbor was in a deal with Kier. He committed suicide.

Prowler2000: Is that true?

Bbaklava: I heard the same thing.

Supertramp11: I can vouch for that.

Aurcadia500: I worked for Kier three years ago. He ridiculed me in front of the entire office just for having a poinsettia plant in my cubicle at Christmas. That guy was the Grinch, Scrooge, and the Bergermeister rolled into one.

Prowler2000: Bergermeister. LOL!!!

Supertramp11: That's true too. Kier was adamant that no time or money be wasted on holiday decorating. He called Christmas decorations "Idiot Glitter."

Hope17: You shouldn't judge him until you've walked in his shoes.

Mojo777: Love to walk in them. Bruno Magli no doubt. And I promise I wouldn't kick anyone. More than Kier would do.

Aurcadia500: Never criticize a man until you've walked a mile in his shoes. That way he can't do anything to you because you're a mile away and you've got his shoes.

Prowler2000: ROFLOL :-D

Kronos345: Wow, Kier had a fan. Hooda thunk?

Prowler2000: Yeah, what's with the fan club, Hope 17? The man was a monster.

Hope17: I'd say you didn't really know him.

Kronos345: Why is it that everyone always tries to make people look better after death? He was what he was.

Supertramp11: Believe what you want, Hope17, Kier's only motivation in life was money. Gain was his only critereon for action, no matter who was hurt, no matter who was left in ashes. Just yesterday he celebrated taking some old man's property. Believe me, I knew Kier—I played squash with him every week for seven years.

Kier's jaw clenched. Supertramp11 was Tim Brey. *That traitorous weasel. I'm going to hand him his head on a platter.* He began to type in a comment, then restrained himself. Brey was on a roll and he wanted to let him dig himself deeper. And he was curious as to the identity of Hope17.

Hope17: This is Sara. And shame on you, Tim. Jim took care of you and your family for more than ten years.

Supertramp11: I'm sorry, Sara, but for your sake not his. Of all people, you had the most to complain about. He made your life a living hell. I know the truth about him serving you the divorce papers. I asked him to wait until after your chemo but he wouldn't.

Hope17: He did some bad things. But he was a good man once. I believe he would have come back someday.

Alleykat9: Like Darth Vader.

Supertramp11: Your loyalty is touching, Sara, but you lost the man you loved long before yesterday. He was dead, Sara. Dead and buried.

Alleykat9: This is like "Days of Our Lives."

Prowler2000: Better.

Mojo777: Is that still on the air?

Hope17: Then I will always love the man he was. I only wish I could have saved him. I would have given anything for that. I would give anything to have the man I married back.

The comments continued for several more pages but Kier just stared at the last entry. How could Sara still care about him after all he had done to her? He walked to the bathroom. Bending low over the sink he splashed his face with water. Then he looked in the mirror. He felt sick to his stomach and angry. But more than anger or even betrayal, he felt something still stronger. He felt shame.

CHAPTER

Eleven

It was nearly noon when Kier walked back down the stairs. Fred was polishing the banister with a dust rag. He looked up at him. "You sure you're not a ghost?"

"Can't prove it."

Fred laughed. "Come back and haunt us again," he said.

Kier walked outside. The air was crisp and fresh. He climbed into his car and drove home.

On the ride down the canyon, Kier mulled over what he'd read. "Heartless," "Monster," "Grinch," "Bergermeister"? His memory had been betrayed by his "friends" as well as his enemies. Only one person seemed to care about him and it was the woman *he'd* betrayed. He was baffled. After all he had done to Sara, she had stood up for him. Why?

He suddenly felt very alone. At least he had Traci. He wondered how she was handling the news. *Probably a wreck*, he thought.

⁕

The roads home were clear and Kier arrived in the valley in less than a half hour. He stopped at a nearby stripmall and picked up a new phone then drove home. He pulled into the driveway, opened the garage door, and parked inside, entering from the garage. He stopped at the edge of the living room. It took him a moment to comprehend what he saw. The room was filled with dozens of shopping bags. Nordstrom, Anthropologie, Lolabella, bebe, White House Black Market; an impressive array. He pulled from one of the bags a black, tufted Gucci bag with the price tag still attached: $3,995.

I guess she decided to cash in while the card was still good. He wondered why she brought everything to his place instead of her own until it occurred to him that she was just being efficient; his place was closer to the malls. He went to the kitchen and called Lincoln.

"How's it going, dead man?" Lincoln said.

"Have you contacted the newspaper yet?"

"No. I had to get Carol to go into the office. But we're just about to serve them."

"Belay that."

"What?"

"I don't want you to contact them yet."

"Why?"

"I don't want anyone to know that I'm alive."

"What have you got up your sleeve, Kier?"

"This is an opportunity, Lincoln. A once-in-a-lifetime opportunity."

"I'm not following you."

"Did you see what Brey wrote on the *Tribune* site?"

"Yeah, I saw that. I'm sorry."

"I'm not. Now I know the truth. For the first time in my life I can see what people really think of me. This is a platinum opportunity."

"Brilliant."

"What are you doing tonight?"

"No plans."

"Let's get a drink at Porcupine Grill. Say, seven?"

"Seven it is."

"See you then." Kier hung up and went back to the front room. He sat down in a wide crushed-velvet chair and lifted his feet up on the ottoman staring at the door while he considered his next move. First Brey, now Traci. He was wondering the best way to handle the two of them when he heard a car pull into the driveway. A moment later came the sound of keys in the deadbolt. The door opened a few inches, then swung open as Traci walked inside, pushing the door open with her rear. Her back was toward him and her arms were threaded through the handles of more shopping bags. She was humming cheerfully. Kier waited for her to set down her bags before he spoke.

"Hi."

She jumped at the sound of his voice and swung around.

"I'd ask where you've been, but I don't need to, do I?"

"James." She held a hand to her chest. "You're . . . what are you doing here?"

"Where should I be?"

"But the paper said . . ."

"I know. I read it." Kier looked over the mountain of shopping bags. "I'm sorry you were so broken up by the news. You must have been devastated."

For a moment she just looked at him, speechless, then recovered. "You know shopping is how I cope with tragedy. It's therapy."

"Looks like group therapy. You must feel like a million bucks. Or is that just how much you spent?"

Her expression relaxed. "Oh, honey, I'm so glad you're okay. What would I have done without you?" She reached out her arms.

"Let's find out. Take your things and go."

"James," she purred, smiling seductively. "C'mon Jimmy."

"And leave the credit card."

Traci pouted. "This isn't fun. Let's celebrate you being alive."

"You've already celebrated my death."

When it was clear he wasn't relenting, her expression changed from seductive to disdainful. She stopped to gather her bags, and lugged the first batch to the door. "Would you give me a hand?"

"No."

"Pig."

It took her six trips to carry everything out to her car. On her last trip he said to her, "The credit card."

She pulled out her wallet, extracted the card and threw it at him. "There." It landed on the floor a few feet from him. "It's true what they say about you. All you care about is money."

He nodded. "Apparently likes do attract."

CHAPTER

Twelve

"You know what they call those things?" Lincoln said to Kier over his second drink, the din of the pub forcing him to speak loudly.

"What things?"

"What the paper did to you."

"Libel."

"Well, besides that. They call them premature obituaries. It's not an erroneous obituary, because everyone's going to have one sometime. It's just premature."

"Yeah, that's profound," Kier said, uninterested.

"It's not the first time it's happened. I looked it up. It's happened to some pretty big names: Paul McCartney, Queen Elizabeth, Ronald Reagan, Mark Twain, Margaret Thatcher. In fact, the death of Pope John Paul II was announced three times.

"The newspapers reported twice that Ernest Hemingway had died. They say that he read a scrapbook of his obituaries every morning with a glass of champagne."

"Didn't Hemingway commit suicide?" Kier asked. He sipped his beer. "Did people trash them too?"

"Of course they did. They were movers and shakers. You can't make omelets without breaking eggs and you've made a lot of omelets my friend."

"Omelets? I'm a freakin' Denny's."

Lincoln laughed. "When do you give Brey the heave-ho?"

"Monday."

"I'd like to see the look on that fool's face when he sees you."

"I'm sure it will be unforgettable."

Lincoln set down his beer. "So how are you doing? Really?"

"I'm okay."

"Good," Lincoln said after a short pause. "That's good."

"You expected otherwise?"

"Well, I wasn't sure. There were some pretty harsh things written about you. And you did just break up with your girlfriend."

"That's a good thing."

"I know. But that doesn't make it any easier. Look what a waste Pam was, and I still gained twenty pounds after she left me."

Kier grinned.

"What?"

"I saw Pam a month after you two separated. I asked how she was doing. She said, 'Great, I just lost two hundred pounds of ugly fat.'"

Lincoln sneered. "Tossing that hen was the smartest thing I've ever done."

"The trick, Lincoln, is to not let what other people think bother you."

"Really, I wish I could do that. Beer helps."

"It's easier when you consider that three percent of the population are certifiably insane. And the rest of them are idiots. Why would you care what idiots think?"

"That's the spirit, old boy," Lincoln said, raising his drink. "To the idiot masses."

Kier looked at Lincoln, his hand wavering with the upheld glass. He raised his own, "To the idiot masses." Both men took a long drink.

CHAPTER

Thirteen

That night Kier had a dream. He was in a spacious hallway with dark-varnished floors and lined with tall, arched windows covered in silk drapes tied back with elegant golden ropes. There were potted orchids and African violets by each window. The ceilings were high, hung with brass and crystal chandeliers, and the walls were covered with an ivory silk. Soft harp music filled the room but he could not see where it was coming from.

The hall was vacant. As he looked around he saw that at the far end of the room was an ornate closed casket made from burled walnut and fastened with copper corner pieces and handles.

He wondered who was inside. He crossed the room but when he reached the casket he was suddenly afraid to look. He lifted the heavy lid. Inside was a woman he knew that he had seen before but didn't recognize until she opened her eyes.

"My son," she said.

"Mom?" She smiled lovingly and a calm feeling came over him.

"My dear, sweet boy. I miss you. We all miss you."

Kier didn't understand. "All?"

"Look and see."

He turned from her to look around the hall, but there was still no one there. He turned back. "I don't . . ." His mother was gone and inside the velvet-lined casket lay Sara. Her skin was a waxlike pallor yet she was still beautiful. Almost involuntarily he spoke her name, "Sara."

At the sound of his voice her eyes opened, looking through him. She spoke and her voice had a sweet, faraway resonance. "Jim, why did you leave me when I needed you the most?"

"I, I . . ." He had no answer. "I'm sorry." His eyes filled with tears. "I really am sorry."

"Me too," she said softly. She looked at him without anger or malice, just sadness.

"Where is everyone?" Kier asked.

She didn't answer but closed her eyes again.

"Sara, come back." He crouched next to the casket. "Sara, where is everyone? Where is Jimmy?" He looked around the room, hoping to see him.

Suddenly an old man entered the parlor. The man stopped near the room's entrance to write in the guestbook. Then, leaning on his walker, he hobbled across the room. As he neared, Kier thought he recognized the man but couldn't remember from where. It took the man several minutes to reach the casket. Without acknowledging Kier, he stood by his side, staring intently at the corpse.

"Thank you for coming," Kier said.

The man turned to look at him. To Kier's surprise there was a gleeful smile on his face. "Wouldn't miss it for the world." Then, turning back to the corpse, his smile changed to a scowl and he spit into the casket. "Rot in hell," he said, wiping his mouth with his sleeve.

Kier turned red with anger and raised his fist. "How dare you. She was a good woman."

"Woman?" the man said.

Kier looked back. His own body was now lying inside the coffin.

"Second best day of my life," the old man mumbled as he hobbled off. "Second best day of my life."

CHAPTER

Fourteen

Kier woke with his heart pounding. He was soaked in sweat and his face was wet with tears. As consciousness flooded back, his chest grew heavy with sorrow. He had lied. He had lied to Lincoln. He had lied to himself. The newspaper article, the Web comments *had* bothered him. Deeply.

How had he come to this place? When had he decided to be *this*? To be hated by strangers as well as those who knew him best, separated from his wife, disowned by his son, and his only friend, Lincoln, his lawyer, was paid a sizable monthly retainer. The truth was, he was more like everyone else than he wanted or pretended to be—he wanted to be loved. He wanted to be missed.

Kier got out of bed, threw his wet shirt on the floor, then headed downstairs. He went through his normal motions, made himself some toast and coffee, went outside and retrieved the newspaper. He sat at the kitchen table eating and reading, less out of interest than to distract his thoughts from his pain. As he thumbed through the pages of the paper he suddenly stopped at the obituaries where a name caught his eye: James Kier. He set down his coffee. Second column to the left, third from the top was his name. Only this time they got it right; it was the other James Kier. There was a small photograph of the man not much larger than a postage stamp. Kier thought he was not an especially good-looking individual. He was balding, his crown covered with a wide comb-over, and his face narrow and homely. Still, there was something about his expression that made him attractive. He looked happy and good-natured. Kier read the obituary.

James A. Kier, "Jak," son of Dick and Bette (Beck) Kier, was born September 26, 1962, in Arcadia, California. He passed away Friday at the age of 47.

James's childhood years were happily spent in California where he excelled at basketball and played on the team that went to the California State finals. He graduated from Arcadia High School in 1979. In April 1982 James was married to the love of his life, Martha Elizabeth Long of Monrovia, California. James moved his family to Utah after his mother took ill and he lovingly took care of her until her death. For more than two decades James worked as a school bus driver for the Wasatch School District and for three years straight was voted "World's Best Driver" by the children. He would remember their birthdays and no child was ever teased or bullied in his presence. His favorite saying was "Not on my bus!" To many children he was their best friend and they would often confide in him their deepest secrets.

James was a great barbecue chef. He enjoyed fishing and spending time with family and friends. James's humble, caring, and sincere ways were felt by all who knew him. He will be missed.

Left to cherish his memory are his wife, Martha, and his three children: Dan Kier and his wife, Linda; Margie Potts and her husband, Joel Eric; and Bonnie Kier. He is also survived by one sister, Ebony Brooke of Pasadena, California.

Preceding James in death were his parents and his brother, Tom.

In his honor, there will be a memorial service at his home (3540 Polk Avenue) on Sunday, at eleven A.M. until noon. Public is invited. The family has requested that in lieu of flowers, a donation be made in James's name to his favorite charity, the Primary Children's Medical Center children's medical fund.

Kier looked down at his watch. It was a quarter to ten. Maybe it had something to do with his dream, maybe not, but for reasons he couldn't fully explain he felt he had to go to this man's memorial service. He tore the article from the paper, then went back upstairs, showered, put on a suit and tie and went to find the other James Kier's home on Polk Avenue.

CHAPTER

Fifteen

Polk Avenue was a dead-end road in a poor section of Rose Park. The small street was lined with cars and Kier had to park a couple of blocks away on a street with run-down and boarded-up houses. He hoped his car would still be there when he got back.

The home of the other James Kier was a tiny, shake-tile-roofed rambler. A plastic Santa Claus with four reindeer perched precariously on the roof. Large, plastic candy canes wrapped with Christmas lights protruded from the snow in the front yard. The house was brown brick with tan and white striped aluminum awnings, surrounded by overgrown pyracantha bushes.

What surprised Kier most were the scores of people—children, teenagers, adults, and the elderly—cued along the walk outside the house, waiting to pay their respects. Kier took his place in the line.

As he waited, he observed three things about the other James Kier. First, the crowd of people who'd come to pay their respects was remarkably diverse in more than just age. The elderly couple behind him was distinguished, the man dressed in a Brioni suit and silk Gucci tie, the woman in a full-length fur coat. From their conversation, he deduced that they were there because the deceased had been kind to their mentally handicapped daughter, who had ridden his bus each day.

"He saved a seat for her next to him at the front of the bus," the woman told someone behind her. "The other kids called it Rachel's seat. Because he respected her they did too."

In contrast, the young man standing in front of Kier might have been sixteen or seventeen and wore a long-sleeved T-shirt in spite of the cold. His hair was dyed black, and he had a pierced ear, pierced nose, and a tattoo of a snake on the back of his neck, partially concealed by dark woven necklaces. He carried a book under his arm; Kier couldn't make out the title.

The second thing he observed was that the young people (and there were many) affectionately referred to the deceased Kier as Jak or Mr. Jimbo.

Third, no matter who they were, or where they were from, there was a palpable sense of loss.

Kier looked around in wonder. *This guy was just a bus driver*, he kept telling himself. The home's interior was as humble as the outside. The carpet, wet from people moving in and out, was a well-worn avocado green shag. The entryway was decorated with Hummel statuary, plastic plants, and cheap prints of *Cats in France*, the kind of art that looked as if it had been purchased at either a garage sale or the clearance table of a Kmart. Above the front door was a hand-painted wooden sign that read *All because two people fell in love*.

It was about half an hour before he

reached the living room where the Kier family stood in a receiving line. A plump, middle-aged woman with a beehive hairdo stood at the front of the line. It was apparent that she was the deceased Kier's wife. The young man standing in front of Kier began to speak. He spoke softly and with a slight lisp likely exacerbated, Kier reasoned, by the stud that protruded from below his lip.

"Mrs. Kier, I wanted to tell you that . . ." The youth suddenly choked up. "Mr. Jimbo saved my life."

She looked at him kindly and took his hand in hers. "Please, tell me about it."

"It was a really bad day. My mom had just left us and I got yelled at by a teacher in front of everyone and then I got beaten up by some football players. Then they shoved me in a garbage can and rolled me through the school's courtyard at lunchtime. I decided I was going to hang myself. As I was getting off the bus, Mr. Jimbo said, 'Hold on there, sport.' He asked me what was wrong. I said 'nothing,' but he looked at me like he knew everything. He said, 'Life sucks sometimes, don't it?' I said, 'Yeah.' He said, 'I know. Sometimes it don't even seem worth living. But you know what, I'm just a bus driver. I'll never be rich. People honk at me all day. No one wants to grow up and be me, but I've got some things worth living for. And so do you.' I started to cry and Mr. Jimbo said, 'You're going to be a great man someday, one that everyone looks up to.' I didn't know what to say. But he did. He asked me if I like to read, I said, 'Yeah mostly fantasy and Sci fi.' He said, 'me too.' Then he gave me the book he was reading. It was *The Hobbit*. He said he thought I would like it.

"From then on we talked every day and we ended up reading the whole *Lord of the Rings* trilogy together. It took us the whole school year. He got me through it." The teenager wiped his eyes.

"So you're Steffan," Mrs. Kier said with a warm smile. "Jim told me so much about you."

The youth said, "I'm here because of him, ma'am."

"Thanks for sharing that with me. We're both going to miss him, aren't we?"

"Sure are, ma'am." He held out the book he carried. "This was his. We had some good talks about it. I'm bringing it back."

She held it close; it was Viktor Frankl's *Man's Search for Meaning*. "This was one of Jim's favorite books," she said. She handed it back to him. "You keep it. I know that's what he'd want."

The youth teared up. "Thank you, ma'am. I'll put it someplace really important. God bless you."

"God bless you, Steffan."

The teenager moved along, wiping his eyes on his shirtsleeve. The woman looked at Kier, then put out her hand. "I'm Martha Kier."

"I'm James."

"Pleased to meet you, James."

"My condolences for your loss."

"Thank you. Jim was one of the good ones God sent to this earth."

Kier suddenly felt a little uncomfortable. "There are a lot of people here."

"He was a simple man, but he touched a lot of lives."

"Well, I'm truly sorry for your loss. Your husband is going to be missed. The world's a little darker place for losing him."

"Thank you for coming."

Kier moved on down the line. The other James had three children, two girls who looked like they were in high school, (even though one of them was married) and a young man about Jimmy's age. He was tall and lanky, with spiky brown hair. He was wearing a navy pin-striped suit that looked too large for him. He stood next to a beautiful young woman who Kier guessed to be his wife. The young man reached out his hand as Kier approached. "I'm Danny."

"I'm sorry for your loss."

"How did you know my father?"

Kier struggled with an answer. "The truth is, I didn't know him all that well. We just crossed paths."

"He was that way, wasn't he? The moment you met him you felt like he was a friend. He was everyone's friend." The young man teared up and his wife put her arm around him. "He was my best friend. I'm lucky to have had him as a father."

Kier looked at him a moment, then said, "More than you know. God bless you."

"Thank you."

Kier walked outside. Even though it was

past noon, people were still arriving and the line was even longer than when he had arrived. Just a bus driver. When he got back to his car he called Linda.

CHAPTER

Sixteen

Linda answered her phone on the second ring. "Hello, Linda Nash speaking."

There was something comforting about hearing her voice. "Hi Linda."

"Who's this?"

"It's Jim."

"Jim who?"

"Your boss, Jim."

She paused. "This isn't funny," she said, and hung up.

Kier pushed the redial button. When she answered he said, "Linda, please don't hang up. It's really me."

"The real James Kier would never say 'please.'" She hung up.

He pressed redial again. She answered on the tenth ring. "Stop calling me," she said angrily. "I don't know what kind of sick joke this is, but I'm going to call the phone company if you call again."

"Look, Linda, it's James Kier and I'm not dead. I can prove it. Ask me something only I would know. Anything."

The voice was his, Linda thought, but the tone was anything but James Kier. "Who was your ten o'clock meeting with Friday morning?"

"My attorney, Lincoln, my wife, Sara, and Steve . . . no, that was before. It was with, uh, Allen. Vance Allen of Scott Homes."

Linda's voice relaxed. "Before that meeting, what was the last thing you said to me?"

He thought back to that morning. "I told you not to talk to Vance. I wanted him on edge."

There was a long pause. "Everyone thinks you're dead. It was all over the news."

"I know. It was a case of mistaken

identity; it was another James Kier who died. I just went to his memorial service."

"This is so weird." She was obviously embarrassed. "I don't know what to say."

"The good news is you don't have to look for a new job." Kier noticed that she didn't say anything. "I guess the bad news is you still have to work for me. I need to meet with you as soon as possible. Can you meet me today?"

"I was on my way to church."

"I can meet with you after church. Please, Linda, it's very important."

"I'll have to bring Mason . . ."

"That's okay. We'll only be a few minutes. Please."

"I get out of church around four. I need to get Max some dinner, but I could come to the office around five-thirty."

"Five-thirty will be great. Just great. Thank you."

In all the years she had worked for him she had never heard him speak this way. It suddenly occurred to her why he was calling.

"If you're going to fire me, you can just do it now."

"Why would I fire you?"

"I just wondered what could be so important that it couldn't wait until tomorrow."

"I'll explain everything when I see you at five-thirty."

"All right. See you then. Goodbye."

Kier flipped up the phone closed. "Thank you," he said to no one. He started his car and drove home.

CHAPTER

Seventeen

Kier was in his office reading freshly posted comments under his article when he heard Linda unlock the building's back door and enter. She was speaking to her son, Mason. "Now don't get into anything. You can sit here and draw. I'll be right out."

"Can I have a can of root beer?"

"Not can, may."

"Can I have a *may* of root beer?"

"No, *may* I have a can of root beer."

"Can I?"

She groaned. "Just a minute."

Kier shut off his computer. The comments on his "obituary" had continued to accumulate, for the most part it was just more of the same kind of attacks. He wasn't sure what drew him to the site; it was like rubbing his tongue over the sharp edge of a cracked tooth. No matter how much it hurt he just couldn't leave it alone.

He heard Linda say, "There's no root beer. I got you a grape soda."

"Okay. Thanks, Mom."

There was a pop as the boy opened the can, then Linda appeared in the doorway, "Good afternoon, Mr. Kier." She wore a crushed velvet burgundy dress and her hair was done up in a simple twist. Kier had forgotten how pretty she was. "Sorry I'm late. Mason's Sunday school teacher stopped me on the way out."

"It's okay. Come in."

She looked pensive as she stepped inside the office. "Did I do something wrong?"

"No, of course not. Would you mind shutting the door?"

"My son is out there . . ."

"Oh, right." Kier stood up and walked to the front of his desk. He motioned to the chair in front of him. "Please, sit down."

She had never heard his voice so gentle; she knew it was irrational but it frightened her. She walked over and sat down in the chair, her body tense with anticipation.

Kier leaned back against his desk, sitting on its edge. "How are you?"

"I'm fine," she said, unconvincingly.

"Are you afraid?"

She looked like she was going to hyperventilate. "A little."

"Thank you for your honesty. Let me get to the point." He looked at her for a moment, then said, "What do you think of me?"

"I beg your pardon."

"It's a straightforward enough question—what do you think of me?"

Straightforward as a minefield, Linda thought. "I think you're good at what you do. Really good."

"And what is it that I do?"

"Develop and manage real estate and other investments."

"Yes, I'm good at that. But what do you think of me as a person?"

She looked down at the ground as she searched for a safe answer. Kier's gaze never left her.

Finally she said, "I don't understand what you're asking me."

"Let's try it this way. What kind of a person am I?" When she didn't look up he rubbed his chin and sighed. "Okay, I'll make this real simple. Am I a good person, a bad person, or somewhere in between?"

Linda carefully picked her words, "You're . . . you're smart . . ."

"Am I the kind of guy you'd, say, want to marry?"

She looked up sharply. "Would I what?"

"Don't be scared. I'm just using the question as a point of reference. If you weren't married, would you want to be married to me?"

"It would be inappropriate," she said.

He smiled. "A safe answer, but not really a truthful one. Because if you really wanted to marry me you wouldn't care, would you?"

She took a deep breath. "Probably not."

"Good." Kier shook his head slowly. "Thank you for being honest." He walked back to his desk, sat down, then picked up a pencil and set it down in perfect alignment with his desk pad. "I know this is hard, but could you be a little more specific? Why wouldn't you want to be married to me? I'm rich. I'm not bad looking. You could do worse."

She looked up at him. "I don't think you would care that much about me. Or my son." Her eyes started to well up with tears. "Please don't fire me, Mr. Kier. You know I need this job."

"I'm not going to fire you, Linda." He leaned back in his chair. "You studied English in college. You know Robert Burns, the poet?"

She nodded. "Of course."

"O wad some power the giftee gie us, to see ourselves as others see us." He looked at her with a strange expression. Linda suddenly wondered if he'd been drinking.

"The truth is, I already knew the answer to the questions I asked you. So let me say what you were afraid to say: You wouldn't want to be married to me because I am selfish and inconsiderate. I would take from you what I wanted and give nothing in return. In short, I would use you. Am I right?"

"I didn't say—"

"Don't worry—this is my confessional, not yours." He paused, looking for the right words. "Do you know why there's a Nobel Peace Prize?"

She stared at him, wondering what this could possibly have to do with their conversation. "No sir."

"It's an interesting story, really, and . . . relevant. Alfred Nobel was the inventor of dynamite. A useful thing, of course. It was used in mining, clearing land—it saved years building the transcontinental railroad. But it was also used in war. People lost their lives. Many, many people.

"As fortune would have it, in 1888, Nobel's brother Emil died. A French newspaper mistook his brother for him and ran an article with the headline, *Le marchand de la mort est mort*, 'The merchant of death is dead.' It went on to say that Dr. Alfred Nobel became rich by finding ways to kill more people faster than ever before. That was the first of many such articles. Nobel was so upset by what he read about himself that he decided to change his legacy. He left his fortune to the establishment of the Nobel Peace Prize."

"I didn't know that."

"It's true." Kier rubbed his chin. "I know, it's a little like a drug dealer leaving his money to a drug rehabilitation clinic. At any rate, Nobel and I have something in common. We've both left a trail of suffering in our wake, and we both got a glimpse of our legacy before we died.

"It's a blessing, really. Painful but not without benefit. It's like seeing your report card while there's still time to change your grade." He looked down for a moment. "I know what you think of me, or at least what you should think of me. I've hurt people. The Bible—yes, I've read the Bible, I was even a deacon once—the Bible says that true religion is to help the widow and the fatherless. I've put them both on the street. I'm like the opposite of true religion. I am not good."

He looked at her, unsure of how she was taking this. Linda sat quietly, her hands laced in her lap. "You don't have to disagree," he said, though she showed no sign of doing so. "No, I'm not a good person. You, on the other hand, are." He leaned forward. "You are kind and forgiving and remarkably selfless. You work forty-five, fifty hours, a week, then go home and take care of your husband and son. I would wager that you couldn't even tell me the last

time you did something just for yourself."
She didn't respond. "You can't, can you?"

"I took a long bath last weekend."

"My point exactly." He stood, then walked
back to her. "That's why I wanted to talk to
you. I need your help."

"What kind of help?"

"We've been together a long time, you
and I. You know more about me than anyone else does. You know just about every
meeting I've ever had, every phone call I've
taken. You know my own clients better than
I do. You send them birthday and wedding
presents with my name on them. I don't
even know if they're married and you send
them flowers on their anniversaries. Am I
right?"

She nodded.

He lowered his voice. "You also know
the people I've hurt, don't you?"

After a moment she nodded. "Yes."

"You've been with me for a long time,
Linda. You've seen me change. Not just
the change in business, but the change in
me. You've seen my son grow up without a
real father. You've seen my marriage fall
apart. Like it or not, you are my life's wit-
ness. That puts you in a unique, if unenvi-

able, position." He crouched down in front of her. "That's why I need your help. I want you to make me a very special list."

Linda raised an eyebrow. "A list?"

"I need the names of everyone I've hurt and my crimes against them. And I need to know where they are now. I want to make it up to them." He looked down for a moment as if the weight of his own words had just fallen on him. "I want to fix things, if possible." He looked back up at her. "Will you help me?"

"When would you like me to start?"

"As soon as possible. I've wasted too much time already."

She thought it over. "I can do that. Anything else?"

"No, I think that's enough for now."

She stood. "Then I'd better get Mason and get home to Max."

Kier got to his feet. He put his hand on her shoulder but quickly removed it as he could see it made her uncomfortable. "Thank you for coming."

"You're welcome, Mr. Kier. I'll see you tomorrow." She walked out of the office and called to her son. "Come on, Mason. It's time to go home."

Kier sat back in his chair and thought about the commitment he had just made. He wondered if he were strong enough to follow through with it.

CHAPTER

Eighteen

Kier arrived at work at his usual time on Monday. As he walked down the hall he was followed by double takes and stares by his employees, their mouths falling open as if they'd seen a ghost. There were even a few audible gasps. He walked directly to Tim Brey's office. Tim was on the phone and froze when he saw him. "I gotta go," he said and dropped the phone into the cradle without waiting for a response from whoever was on the other end of the call.

"Hi, Tim."

Brey stared at him speechless.

"What's up?"

"I don't understand," Brey said.

"Understand what?" Kier was enjoying this.

"The paper said you were . . ."

"Dead? I know. I read it. Then I checked my pulse and concluded it was just poor reporting."

"Oh, thank God."

Kier rubbed his hands together and approached Brey's desk. "Really? Because I would think from what you wrote that you weren't really all that happy working for me."

Brey turned pale. "What are you talking abo—"

Kier lifted his hand and stopped him. "Please, Tim, don't insult me." He reached into his pants pocket and fished out the comments he'd printed out that morning, and read: "Kier's only motivation in life was money. Gain was his only criterion for action, no matter who was hurt, no matter who was left in ashes. Just yesterday he celebrated taking some old man's property. Believe me, I knew Kier—I played squash with him every week for seven years." Kier looked back up at Brey. "Did you want to add anything to that, Supertramp?"

Brey stared at him in horror, "So is this where you throw me under the bus?"

Kier smiled. "Saturday I might have. Wanted to. Actually, I was kind of looking forward to it. But I've had time to think. There was some truth to what you wrote. More than I wanted to hear, but I needed to hear it. So I came in to thank you."

Brey looked at him skeptically. "Now you're insulting *me*. Go on, get it over with."

"No, I'm serious. I owe you." Kier put his hands in his pockets. "I just wanted to let you know that I'm going to be working at home for a while on a project."

"What kind of project?"

"A *special* one. Let everyone know that the news of my death was premature. I'm sure that will ruin their week but they'll get over it. I don't know how long I'll be out, but I trust that you'll run things with your usual efficiency."

"Yes, sir."

"Good man." He started to go but stopped at the doorway. "Oh, and Brey, get someone to put up a tree or something."

"What kind of tree?"

"A Christmas tree. You know, deck the halls, that sort of thing. Christmas is only three weeks away. From the looks of things you'd never even know it was the season."

"Yes, sir."

"Good man."

Brey sat stunned, as Kier walked out of his office.

CHAPTER

Nineteen

Kier smiled at Linda as he passed her going into his office.

"Good morning, Linda."

"Good morning, Mr. Kier," she replied awkwardly. His changed demeanor was still unnerving to her. A few minutes later she paged him. "Mr. Kier?"

"Yes?"

"May I come in?"

"Of course."

A moment later, she stepped inside his office carrying a file folder. "I'm done."

"Done?"

She walked up to his desk. "With the *list*."

"You've finished it already?"

"It's all right here. . . ."

He took the folder from her. "I didn't expect it so soon."

"The people on it were never that far from my mind."

Kier opened the file and glanced inside. There were five names on the memo, each with their own page and a brief description of their circumstances. He was surprised to see so few names. He looked back up at her. "Only five?"

"Think of them as the finalists."

"Finalists?"

"Mr. Kier, if you want a list of all the people you've hurt or offended, I'll drag in the file cabinet." Linda herself was surprised at her own forwardness. "I'm sorry. These are the ones who would keep me up at night."

"Fair enough," Kier said. He read their names aloud.

Celeste Hatt
Eddie Grimes
Estelle Wyss

David Carnes
Gary Rossi

"I put their contact information under their briefs."

He thumbed through the attached pages. "The first one here, Celeste Hatt—there's no contact information."

"That's because I can't locate her. But I'll keep trying."

Kier continued reading.

"When are you going to start?" Linda asked.

Kier looked up. "Tomorrow morning. I'll be working at home for the next few weeks, Tim knows and I expect between you and him things will run smoothly. If you need anything signed, just bring it by the house. On second thought, why don't you just come by the house every day. Say, around four."

"Okay. Do you need anything else?"

He closed the folder. "No, that's all for now."

She turned to leave.

"Linda."

"Yes?"

"Thank you."

She smiled cynically. "Tell me that after you've seen them," she said and walked out of his office.

✦

Kier opened the folder again and looked at the list. Five names. Five damaged lives. Five lives connected to his own. It was his plan to reach each of these people before Christmas and make things right. This was his Christmas list.

CHAPTER

Twenty

Eddie Grimes

Former owner of Grimes Construction. You forced him out of business and into personal bankruptcy. His current residence: 657 Gramercy Avenue, Salt Lake City.

An inversion had settled into the valley, leaving the air brown and thick. Kier sat in his car with the heater on, Linda's list in the folder on his lap. While visiting these people and doing what he could to make things right had seemed a good idea in theory, sitting in his car outside the home of the first of his visits cast his plan in a different light. According to Linda he had ruined these people's lives. What kind of reception could he expect?

He looked again at the name before him: Eddie Grimes. He didn't need to read the file to remember the man or what he had done to him. Grimes had once owned Grimes Construction, a small but well-regarded and profitable local construction firm that was growing quickly. Grimes had bid against Kier on a large development and won the job. Kier didn't need the work—in fact he was struggling to keep up with his own workload—but he was angry at losing the project and threatened by the success of the upstart competitor. Kier decided to squash the burgeoning company. With the information he had gathered in the project's bidding process and his knowledge of the market, he knew that there was a problem with the availability of certain supplies, especially drywall.

With his substantial cash reserves Kier bought up all the drywall in the Rocky Mountain area, enough to stock his next three projects and, in the short run, to create a regional shortage. When it was time for Grimes to order the needed material, there was none to be had in the state or any of the surrounding areas. The soonest he could find was more than thirty days out. Grimes's project was brought to a complete standstill, costing him substantial late fees and overhead each day his crew sat idle. Another contractor, also caught in Kier's manufactured shortage, informed him of Kier's purchase. As humiliating as it was, Grimes went to Kier to ask him to sell him some of his drywall. Kier not only refused, but berated Grimes for his poor planning, calling him a "donkey among thoroughbreds."

As his losses grew, Grimes was forced to lay off his workers and to eventually abandon the project altogether at a huge financial loss, forcing his company into bankruptcy. Also lost was his reputation. With such a public failure, no one would work with Grimes Construction again.

The development was awarded to Kier, who not only capitalized on Grimes's completed work, but raised his price to complete the job, forcing the investors to pay nearly 20 percent more than his original bid. Kier bought himself a villa in Palm Springs to celebrate the project's completion.

Pouring salt on the wound, Kier named the back road leading to the development's garbage Dumpsters "Grimes Street."

At the height of his success, Grimes had built himself an eight-thousand-square-foot home on the east bench of the valley. Kier had driven by it with Sara. She gasped when she saw it. Though Kier wouldn't admit it, he was also impressed. It was a beautiful French château-style house impeccably landscaped with cobblestone walks, statuary, and potted kumquat trees lining the front walk. Kier could only assume that the home was lost with everything else. The house Kier now sat in front of was a far stretch from what he'd seen before. This place was small and badly in need of repair; ironic, Kier thought, for a homebuilder.

What do you say to a man you've destroyed? Kier wondered. *How could he make things right?* As he considered his dilemma he had an idea. Kier's company could use the talents of a building contractor as skilled as Grimes. He could offer him a top-level position, eventually even stock options. And even better, the extra 20 percent Kier had made from the sabotaged project would more than cover the cost of hiring Grimes. He suddenly felt good about the meeting; they'd work something out. *Who knows,* he thought, *by afternoon they might be laughing and swapping stories.*

Kier climbed out of his car, walked to the

gate in the chain link fence, and let himself in. The walk leading up to the front porch had not been shoveled. The curtains in the front windows were drawn and the only indications that there was life inside the house were the paw prints in the snow of a large dog leading to and from the front door.

Kier trudged through the snow and climbed three steps to the porch. There were two pairs of skis leaning against the house. Kier pushed the doorbell. He didn't hear anything so he rapped on the door with the back of his hand. His knock was answered by the low, menacing growl of a dog that soon erupted into fierce barking. A minute later the doorknob turned. A pretty teenage girl with short brown hair that perfectly framed her face opened the door. She wore ear buds that ran down her shirt. She positioned herself between the excited dog and the narrow slot between the door and the doorjamb. With the door open the dog barked even more fiercely.

"Is this the Grimes residence?"

She pulled a white earbud from her ear. "Sorry, what?"

"Do the Grimeses live here?"

"Yes."

"Is your father here?"

The girl, still struggling with the dog, grimaced. "Yeah, but he's watching TV."

The dog pushed its nose past the girl. It was a large black and brown German shepherd, its teeth bared. Kier watched somewhat anxiously as the small young woman strained to push the dog back. "Stop it, Samson. Sit! Sit!"

"Do you think I could speak with him?" Kier asked.

"I think so. I'll see." She reached back for the dog, then stepped back from the door, pulling the dog by its choke collar. "C'mon, Samson." Even with her commands the dog strained against her. "C'mon, stupid dog." She left Kier alone on the porch with the door open. Kier looked inside. The room was simply furnished but tidy. There was a large family picture of Grimes, his wife, and three children. On the side wall was a Catholic icon with candles and a large picture of Jesus with an exposed heart. He could hear a distant conversation.

"Dad, someone's here for you."

"Who is it?"

"Some man," the girl replied.

A moment later Eddie Grimes appeared

from the darkened hallway, wearing a San Francisco 49ers T-shirt and denim jeans. At first he just stared, not recognizing Kier. It was evident when he realized who was at his door. "What are you doing here?"

"Eddie, I came to—"

"You came to what?" He shouted angrily. He walked up to the door. "What are you doing on my property?"

"I just came to—" He didn't get another word off. Grimes threw a punch to Kier's face, connecting with Kier's nose and knocking him backward off the porch and down the stairs. He landed on his back on the snow-covered walk below, smacking his head on the surface. Kier saw stars and had there not been a couple feet of snow on the ground the fall likely would have knocked him out. A flash of pain shot up his leg. He groaned as he looked up, wet, aching, and dazed. Grimes was standing above him on the porch, red-faced. "I told you if I ever saw you again . . ." He let off a string of curses in machine-gun fashion. Kier put his hand to his nose. It was bent at a slight angle and when he drew his hand away it was covered in blood.

"Eddie, listen . . ."

"I'll give you five seconds to get off my property before I break you into a million pieces."

"I just wanted . . ."

"I don't care what you want. No one cares what you want." He turned back toward the house. "Lucy! Let Samson out."

"But Dad . . ."

"I said let him out!"

Kier struggled to his feet. "Eddie . . ."

Grimes was made even more furious at his daughter's refusal to release the dog. While Kier struggled to his feet, Grimes went back inside, emerging a moment later holding the dog by its choke collar. The dog strained against his grip, worked up by his master's shouting. "Get him, Samson. Sick 'em. Tear the bum's legs off."

The dog lunged wildly against Grimes's grip. Kier staggered backward toward the gate, searing pain shooting up his leg with each step. Then the dog pulled loose. Forgetting his pain, Kier turned and ran the last few yards to the gate, slamming it shut behind him. The dog bounded through the snow and smashed against the gate, its body bouncing off the chain link. The dog was just inches from Kier, snarling and frothing at the mouth.

Grimes stood on his porch shouting and shaking his fist. "If I ever see you on my property again, you're dog meat, Kier. Dog meat! You stinkin' . . ."

Kier didn't hear his final words as he had climbed inside his car. He wiped the blood from his face with his sleeve, then started his car and drove off.

CHAPTER

Twenty-one

As instructed, Linda arrived at Kier's house at four o'clock that afternoon. She pushed the doorbell; Kier answered on the intercom.

"Who is it?"

"It's me, Linda." She paused. "You sound different. Are you okay?"

"Yes."

"I brought some papers you need to sign."

"Just sign them yourself. You can forge my signature."

"You know I don't do that."

There was a long hesitation before he

relented. "The door's unlocked. Let yourself in."

She pushed open the door and stepped inside, stopping in the foyer to remove her coat. "Where are you?"

"In the living room."

She gasped when she saw him, "Omigosh . . ." Kier was lying on the couch. His nose had been set and bandaged and he had a bag of frozen peas on his forehead. His braced ankle was elevated on a stack of pillows. Both eyes were blackened. She quickly walked to him.

"What happened?"

"Grimes wasn't all that happy to see me. Or maybe he was. I'm not sure."

"He hit you for apologizing?"

Kier grimaced. "I didn't get that far."

"What can I do for you?"

"You can get me another cold pack from the refrigerator."

Linda lay her coat and the documents on the coffee table in front of the couch and went to the refrigerator, returning a moment later holding a blue cold pack and a bag of succotash. "Do you want the ice pack or the vegetables?"

"I'll try the ice pack."

She sat down next to him, lifted the bag of peas, then gently laid the ice pack on the bridge of his nose. "Maybe this wasn't such a good idea."

"It was a great idea. One of my best."

She couldn't tell if he was being facetious. "Maybe you could just phone everyone . . . or write a nice note."

"I destroyed their lives and you think I should write them a note?"

"It would be safer."

"I can't argue with that."

"It's a good thing he didn't have a gun."

"He didn't need one. He had a dog."

"Exactly. So you'll write notes?"

"No."

She stood, shaking her head at his stubbornness. "It's your funeral."

"No, I've been to my funeral. This isn't so bad."

"The documents are right there—on the table. There's a drywall contract for the Bunten job and Tim Brey needed you to sign off on the development contract for the Allen property."

"I'll look at that later." He adjusted the icepack. "How is Brey?"

Linda grinned. "Like a death row inmate

with a commuted execution date. I think he's waiting for the old James Kier to return."

"Good. It will keep him humble. Did he decorate the place?"

"Decorate?"

"Decorate, for Christmas."

She smiled. "Yes. It looks nice. Thank you."

"You're welcome."

"Oh, Robyn at Le Jardin called this morning. Someone wants to rent the Garden Reception area on New Year's Day. But they want a discount.

"Robyn knows we don't do that."

"She knows. But in this case she thought she should ask."

"I pay her not to bother me with these details."

"It's for your son's wedding."

Kier lifted the cold pack to look at her. "Jimmy? Why didn't he call me?"

"According to Robyn, the bride and her mother chose the place. She was pretty certain that they didn't know you owned it."

"But Jimmy does . . ." He lay back down. "He doesn't plan to invite me."

"You don't know that," Linda said.

Kier sighed. "Yes, I do." He closed his eyes. After a moment he said, "When I went to the other James Kier's memorial service I met his son. He said his father was his best friend. Mine doesn't even want me to come to his wedding. How could I have gone so wrong?"

Linda didn't say anything.

"Tell Robyn to just give them the place. The catering, flowers, everything they need."

"I'll call." She put her coat back on. "So now what?"

"Back to the list."

"Who's next?"

"The Wysses."

"The Wysses," she said thoughtfully. "Estelle's in her eighties. At least you know she can't beat you up."

"After what I did, she still might try."

"Well, keep your guard up this time. I think you can take her."

He smiled in spite of his pain. "Thanks."

"I'll put the peas back in the freezer. Would you like me to get you something for dinner?"

"No. I've got instant noodles in the cupboard."

"Noodles. Great. Call if you need any-thing else. Good night."

"Good night."

She stopped at the edge of the room. "Mr. Kier?"

"Yes?"

"I know your first visit didn't exactly go the way you hoped. But I'm proud of you anyway."

He looked at her. "At least someone is."

"I'll see you tomorrow."

She let herself out. Kier held the ice-pack closely to his nose. *Why didn't you call me, Jimmy?*

CHAPTER

Twenty-two

Lincoln walked past Kier as he meandered through the steak house, looking for him. Kier called out, "Hey, lawyer."

Lincoln looked directly at Kier but still didn't recognize him, which was not surprising, since Kier wore a Yankees cap and sunglasses perched gingerly above his bandaged nose.

"You're late."

He looked at Kier quizzically. "Excuse me?"

"Lincoln, it's me, Kier."

Lincoln stared at him. "Good heavens, man. What happened to you?"

"Accident."

"What kind of accident?"

"An accidental accident. Quit gawking. You look like a trout."

Lincoln sat down, still staring at him.

"So what's the difference between a lawyer and a bucket of pond scum?" Kier asked.

"What happened to you?"

"You have to answer first."

"The bucket."

Kier frowned. "Try this one. You're stranded on an island with Hitler, a lawyer, and Attila the Hun. You have a gun with only two bullets, what do you do?"

"Shoot the lawyer twice. Enough, already. What did you do? What happened?"

"I knew it would happen someday," Kier said seriously.

"You knew this would happen?"

"I knew I'd run out of jokes."

Lincoln drew forward. "Kier, give me a straight answer. What are you up to?"

"What makes you think I'm up to something?"

"You mean besides the fact that you look like Mike Tyson's sparring partner?

I've known you a long time, Kier. I can hear the cogs turn in that head of yours."

"All right, I'll tell you. Just don't freak out on me." He leaned back. "I had Linda compile a list of people I've hurt. I'm going to see them all before Christmas."

"Is that what happened? You went to see one of them?"

"Yes."

"Man, have you lost your mind?"

"No, I want to make things right."

"As your lawyer, I strenuously advise against this."

Kier lifted his glass. "Strenuously? That sounds serious."

"Just look in the mirror, man. You never apologize after a car accident; it creates an expectation of guilt. What if these people decide to sue you? Or worse."

"What's worse?"

"Break your face."

"Could happen," Kier said.

Lincoln shook his head. "You *have* lost it. You've finally lost it."

"I've lost worse," Kier said. "So, as a human being as opposed to a lawyer, what do you think of what I'm doing?"

"I think you're out of your freaking mind."

"No really, Lincoln, don't hold back."

"Listen, Jim, I know what you're doing. You read all those comments about you on the Internet and you've had a sudden flare-up of conscience. Am I right?"

"Maybe."

"I know I'm right. The same thing happened to me when Pam left me. But you know what I did?"

"Got drunk for a week?"

"Well, after that. I did nothing. And I'm glad I did. Let me tell you, just ride it out. The guilt will go away. I promise."

"That's what I'm afraid of." Kier rolled his glass between his hands. "What happens when it doesn't bother me anymore?"

"Then you sleep well."

"I've hurt people, Lincoln."

"And people have hurt you. It's a big fat give-and-take. It's what makes the world go round." As he leaned back his eyes narrowed. "You need to tell me who did this. I can have them taken care of. I have friends in low places."

"You're not going to do anything. This is nothing compared to what I did to him."

"Good, so you got a few pokes in."

"That's not what I meant. This is about restitution, not retribution."

"No, this is now about retribution. Was it Gifford? Park? Shelton? How about Pinnock or Mitchell? Or that Johnson guy over at Plastiform."

Kier shook his head. "It's pathetic that it took you all of two seconds to come up with your own list of people who hate me and none of them are on *my* list. It just proves my point."

"What point?"

"That I deserved this."

"Listen, Kier, if you're going to make omelets you've got to break some eggs. And you, my friend, are a master chef."

"Enough of the omelet thing."

At that moment the server walked up to the table. "You gentlemen ready?"

"Get me a raspberry pilsner," Lincoln said.

"You betcha. Anything else for you?" she asked Kier.

"I'm fine with Coke."

"Great. I'll be right back with your drinks." She walked off.

Lincoln reached down into his attaché. "By the way, I brought the divorce papers. Sara's signed them." He laid them on the table and Kier looked at his wife's signature.

"Not now, Lincoln."

"It will take just a few seconds. Just sign where I put the Post-its and it's over."

"I'm not sure that's what I want."

"What do you mean?" Lincoln looked at him.

"I'm just not so sure about this anymore. Do you know what hurts the most right now?"

"From the looks of it I'd say your nose."

"What I did to Sara. She's the one I feel the worst about. I can't get her off my mind. I left her when she needed me the most. What kind of a man does that?"

"People grow apart, Jim. It happens."

"Growing has nothing to do with it. I've fallen, and I don't know how to get back to her. I don't even know where to begin."

"Well, at least you won't have to worry about it for long."

Kier glared at him.

"What?" Lincoln said.

Kier stood, pushed back his chair. "I've got to go. He took out a ten-dollar bill and threw it on the table, then walked away.

"Come on, Kier. What'd I say?"

CHAPTER

Twenty-three

Standing in front of the mirror, Kier slowly pulled off his bandage. His nose was still swollen, his left eye was puffy and black, his other a dull collage of purple, green, and yellow. For a minute he just looked at himself. "How many people have wanted to do that to you?" He put the bandage back on.

He took his phone out of his pocket. He looked at it for a moment, then pushed speed dial. A woman whose voice he didn't recognize answered. "Kier residence."

"Is Sara there?"

"I'm sorry, she's not available right now. May I take a message?"

"Who is this?"

"This is Beth, Sara's sister. May I take a message?"

Beth was Sara's only sister and Steve's mother. Kier hoped Steve hadn't told her about how he'd treated him through the divorce's legal wrangling but guessed he had. "This is James."

"Jim," she said coolly. "You don't sound like Jim."

"I've got . . . a cold."

"What do you want?"

"I *want* to talk to Sara."

"Over my dead body," she said coldly.

"That would be nice, Beth, but it's beside the point. I need to talk to Sara."

"No, you can't."

"You can't stop me. She's my wife."

"Since I'm holding the phone, yes I can stop you, and no, she's not your wife. At least not anymore. You've been pretty clear about that."

She had a point about the phone. "Come on, Beth, just let me talk to her."

"Haven't you hurt her enough? You just

leave her alone." Beth slammed down the phone.

Kier flipped his cell phone shut. *Now what?*

CHAPTER

Twenty-four

The first notable sign of Sara's cancer had surfaced in early March as a sudden, sharp pain in her lower abdomen. It wasn't the first symptom she'd experienced; for several months she had felt fatigued and lost weight but she didn't think much of it. Her husband had just left her. Stress does awful things to the body.

It wasn't until after three weeks of recurrent stomach pain that she went to her family doctor to find out what was wrong. He ran a series of tests, then called her three days later to tell her that he had scheduled more tests with a colleague of his who was an oncologist. It was still another week before she had a conclusive diagnosis—stage three pancreatic cancer. The prognosis wasn't good. Dr. Halestrom, the oncologist, explained to her that the cancer had spread beyond the pancreas to major blood vessels and lymph nodes, so surgery wasn't an option. Alone with a doctor she'd only met once before, Sara broke down. The doctor let her cry, then said, "There's always hope."

Sara wiped her eyes. "Have you ever seen someone with cancer this advanced cured?"

From the doctor's hesitation she knew the answer before he spoke. "No. I'm sorry."

After a few more minutes, her crying slowed then stopped. She looked up, calm. This had always been her way: when her mother died, when her husband left her. Get the crying out of the way, then get down to business. "How long do I have?"

"It's hard to say. I've seen people—"

"Your best guess."

"If we aggressively treat the cancer with a combination of radiation and chemotherapy, six months to a year."

"If I don't?"

"Maybe three."

"That's not a lot of time," she said, as if she were talking about a warranty on a washing machine instead of her life. "But, there's a chance I could make it to my son's wedding." Something felt hopeful about that. Her son would be starting a new life and a new family, starting the cycle anew. Cancer or not, her role would diminish in his life. It would be like the changing of acts in a play. The timing, if not perfect, was at least appropriate.

"When is your son's wedding?"

"New Year's Day."

"It's certainly possible."

"Then let's do it. What do I do now?"

"We schedule your chemotherapy and radiation."

"How soon can we start?"

"I can schedule the first radiation treatment next week. It will help if you have someone to go through this with." He looked at the ring on her hand. "Are you married?"

She tried to keep her voice steady. "He left me a couple months ago."

"I'm sorry. Do you have any other family? Friends?"

"My son. But he's away at college." She took a deep breath. "There's my sister."

"You should give her a call."

✧

Sara's treatments began the following week. Her sister, Beth, drove her to her first radiation treatment. She went in at six in the morning and came home the same afternoon, weak and nauseated. As Beth helped her from her car, a silver Toyota Corolla pulled up in the driveway behind her. A young man with short red hair and wearing Weejuns, corduroy jeans, and an oxford button-down shirt climbed out.

"Mrs. Kier?" he said, his eyes darting back and forth between the two women.

Beth didn't know what the young man wanted but intuitively sensed it couldn't be good. "You stay away from her. Mrs. Kier is very sick."

He walked up and handed Sara an envelope. "Sorry. You've been served."

If Beth hadn't been supporting her sister she likely would have slapped the man. "You have some nerve, you wimpy little mouse, I hope—"

"Beth," Sara said.

"You're a terrible person!" Beth yelled at

him. "And you're ugly, you four-eyed carrot-top creep. How do you sleep at night?"

The young man ran wide-eyed back to his car and quickly drove away.

When Sara was in her bed she asked Beth to read the letter.

Beth resisted. "No, honey, it's not important. It can wait."

"I need to know."

Beth reluctantly opened the envelope and read the letter in silence.

"What is it?" Sara asked.

"Honey . . ."

"Jim's divorcing me."

Beth exhaled. "The louse . . ."

Sara closed her eyes and for the first time that day she cried. "I thought he would come back," she said. "I was sure he'd come back."

"I told you, Sis, he's lost his soul." Beth cradled her sister's head. "I'm so sorry, baby. I'm so sorry."

For the rest of the evening Sara lay in bed sick in body and heart. Though she never said it out loud, for the first time since her diagnosis she was glad she was dying.

Eight months later, Thanksgiving was Sara's last attempt at normality. With much

effort and pain she created a simple Thanksgiving dinner for her, Jimmy, and Juliet.
But after preparing the meal she was so
exhausted and sick that she wasn't able to
eat. She feared that Jimmy might finally
be suspecting the truth of her condition
but she did her best to allay his fears. "It's
just the side effect of the treatments," she
told him. "Dr. Halestrom said it would be
this way."

Jimmy didn't know that she had already
made her funeral arrangements. To Sara it
wasn't a question of *if*, only when. Could
she live to see her son married? It was her
will versus the cancer, and each day she
lost a little ground. If she was strong enough,
she could win the battle. But she already
knew who would win the war.

CHAPTER

Twenty-five

Estelle Wyss

Estelle and Karl Wyss. Estelle was a friend of Sara's: from church. You entered a deal with the Wysses using their land as collateral. When things went bad they took the loss. They still live in the back of the Il Pascolo subdivision. I'm sure you remember where that is.

It had been many years—he couldn't remember how many exactly, but more than a decade—since Kier had driven through Il Pascolo, Italian for "the pasture." The name of the development was Estelle Wyss's idea. Estelle Zito Wyss was second-generation Italian, though she never actually set foot on *terra Italiana* until her late twenties when she was on her honeymoon. It was everything she had fantasized. She never wanted to leave the country and forever afterward referred to herself as a "displaced" Italian. From then on she and her husband, Karl, spent most of their summers in Genoa or near Lake Como or sometimes south along the Windex blue waters of the Amalfi coast.

The pretentious development was designed to evoke the Italian countryside; its entrance was marked by a gargantuan round stone from an authentic olive press (from California, not Italy) and an Italian fresco painted on the entrance's stucco wall, flanked on both sides by grapevine-covered trellises.

Under Kier's direction the homes had been marketed as villas—overpriced, stucco-slathered homes built on lots barely large enough to accommodate them. The streets all had Italian names: *Via Masaccio, Santa Maria del Fiore, Giuseppe Garibaldi, Via Di Sera, Bagno a Ripoli*; names difficult to pronounce and even harder to spell, forevermore the bane of every homeowner who moved to the subdivision.

Three blocks from the entrance, at the furthest end of the development, was a house that didn't fit in with the others. It was a small red-brick ranch that looked more like it belonged in Tulsa than Tuscany. The only thing Italian about the home was the faded tricolor flag that hung from the garage and a sign in the driveway that read, PARKING FOR ITALIANS ONLY. It was ironic that the only house that didn't look indigenous to the development was the only one that was. It was the Wysses' original home and at one time all sixty-four acres of Il Pascolo had belonged to them.

The first time Kier saw the Wysses' property it was an operating dairy with more than a hundred black and white Holsteins contentedly roaming the grounds. Estelle Wyss had told Sara that she and Karl were getting too old to run the dairy and, unable to compete with the larger, more high-tech dairy operations, were looking at selling or developing the land. Unlike her husband, Karl, a Swiss immigrant, Estelle had never liked the dairy life (too many flies and cow pies, she told Sara) and looked forward to finally fulfilling her dream of retiring to the northern Italian countryside. It was because of Kier that her dream never came true.

Kier recognized the underdeveloped land in the middle of an established suburb as a rarity and, a gold mine. Kier convinced the trusting couple that rather than selling their property outright, they would make money faster by leveraging their property against the development. Spurred by greed, Kier rushed the construction, wagering with the Wysses' property. Kier built more than two dozen spec homes and waited for them to sell; the venture couldn't have been more poorly timed. As the homes were nearing completion, the local real estate market took a sudden plunge and the homes sat, overpriced and unsold. When the construction loans came due, the Wysses lost everything except their own home and three quarter-acre lots they had excluded from the deal near the back of the development. Also lost was Sara and Estelle's friendship.

As Kier sat in his car rehearsing his speech, he glanced at himself in the car's rearview mirror. It had been a decade since he'd seen the Wysses and they were unlikely to recognize him even without his black eyes and bandage. He took a deep breath, climbed out of his car, and hobbled up to the house. Blue grains of ice melt had been scattered the length of the shoveled walk, like seeds sown into the packed ice. Above the door was a painted plaster sign: *La Vita è Bella*.

Kier knocked and a woman's voice sang out, "Just a minute." A moment later an elderly woman dressed in a colorful knit sweater and blue jeans opened the door. Kier recognized her immediately. Estelle Wyss's hair had turned gray, and she had new wrinkles, but the bright eyes and smile were the same. She looked at the bandaged man suspiciously but still managed to smile warmly. "May I help you?"

"Mrs. Wyss, you probably don't recognize me with the bandage."

She squinted. "I'm sorry, my eyesight is a little fuzzy today. Sometimes my diabetes will do that. Are you the new fellow from the congregation?"

"I'm James Kier."

She repeated slowly, "James . . . Kier . . ." Her smile faltered. "Mr. Kier. What can I do for you?"

"I was wondering if we could talk."

"I was just about to take my afternoon nap."

"I'm sorry to bother you. I won't take

much of your time, just a few minutes. Please."

She hovered over a decision, then exhaled as she acquiesced. "All right. Come in."

"Thank you."

He stepped inside the house; it smelled of linen and baked bread. Even with the passing of so many years he remembered his visits to the home and how warmly he'd been received. Like the home's exterior, nothing much had changed. The heavy oak kitchen table was still there, the one they had all sat around that evening, eating chocolate and anise pizzelles, as Kier explained his plans, the Wysses holding hands and listening eagerly. There had been excitement back then, and smiles and laughter. Now the memories turned on him. He felt like he was returning to a crime scene.

Estelle Wyss motioned to the living room. "Please, have a seat."

Her cordial welcome was not what he expected, especially after his experience with Grimes. "Thank you." He sat down in a floral upholstered armchair.

Estelle sat down across from him, her arms folded. "How is Sara?"

"Not well. She has pancreatic cancer."

She looked genuinely sorrowful. "I'm sorry to hear that. I'm sure you're taking good care of her."

Kier didn't answer.

"I'd like to talk to her. It's been so long. Too long."

"I know she'd like that. She was very upset about what happened . . ."

Mrs. Wyss did not react to his reference to the past. "So what can I do for you?"

"Is your husband here?"

"Karl passed away four years ago."

"I'm sorry."

"So am I. He was a good husband and a good man." She gazed at Kier expectantly. "What do you need from me, Mr. Kier?"

"Mrs. Wyss, I came to apologize."

"For?"

The question surprised him. "For what I did."

"And what would that be?"

She seemed genuinely unaware; the thought crossed his mind that she'd actually forgotten his part in the loss of her property and it might be better to not answer her in-quiry. Then again, maybe she just wanted to hear him say it. "For losing your land."

"Oh, that."

"The thing is . . ." As much as he had rehearsed his speech in his head, he was suddenly at a loss for words. He looked at her awkwardly. "The thing is, I didn't mean to hurt you."

"No, I suppose you didn't. But more im-portantly, you didn't mean not to."

The words stung. Neither spoke. Then Estelle asked, "Are you dying?"

"No." He shook his head. "No, I'm not."

"So what is your intent, Mr. Kier? Are you seeking my forgiveness? Are you look-ing to make amends?"

"Yes. Both."

She nodded. "Well, I've already forgiven you. Years ago. You see, I don't hold on to the wrongs done to me; they're just ballast for the soul. Jesus admonished us to for-give *all* men, seventy times seven. Not just the penitent ones.

Her voice lowered. "It was more difficult for Karl to forgive you, but in his last year I think he found peace as well. And as far

as amends, I don't see that there is anything you can do."

Kier swallowed. "There must be *something*."

"Even if it were in your power to return
our land, it would be of no use to me. I
wouldn't know what to do with it. That time
has passed."

"How about your dream of living in Italy?
I could make that happen."

"With someone else's loss? No, I couldn't
do that."

"No, no—I have . . . legitimate profits. I
could pay for it."

She smiled sadly. "There was a time
when I might have taken you up on your
offer, Mr. Kier, but not now. I'm too old and
the doctors have me too well tethered to
the local medical establishment. And without Karl, the dream wouldn't be the same
anyway.

"So you see, Mr. Kier, you can't make
amends. You can't give me back my land.
You can't give me back my health. You can't
give me back my husband and you can't
give me back my dreams. You certainly
can't give me back my innocence."

Her words washed over him like a wave, leaving him floundering. "Is there anything I *can* give you back?"

She smiled at him sadly. "Yes, Mr. Kier. My afternoon."

"Of course." He stood. "I'm very sorry."

"I know."

He walked back to his car and climbed inside. His visit to Eddie Grimes had been less painful.

CHAPTER

Twenty-six

As Kier started his car he glanced down at his cell phone. There were two missed calls. The first was from his office. Linda, he guessed, as Brey was still afraid to call him. It took him a moment to recognize the second number; he hadn't gotten a call from Sara for some time.

Seeing the number filled him with mixed emotions, but to his own surprise, mostly gladness. He immediately dialed the number. Sara answered on the seventh ring. "Hello."

"Hi. It's Jim." When she didn't speak he added, "I'm returning your call."

"I didn't think I'd hear from you so soon, Jim. Actually, I didn't think I'd hear from you at all. I was calling to tell you that Juliet got a call from Le Jardin."

"Who?"

"Juliet. Our son's fiancée."

Kier silently berated himself. "Of course. Sorry."

"She said they're going to let them use the facility for free. Was that your doing or Robyn's?"

"Do you really need to ask?"

"Yes."

"It was me," he replied. "Why didn't Jimmy just call me?"

"When was the last time you talked to your son?"

"Fair enough."

"Juliet wanted me to thank you."

"Tell her she's welcome."

"You should tell her yourself."

"She should thank me herself."

"You're right," Sara said. "I'll tell her."

Neither of them spoke for a moment. He scrambled for something to say. "I just saw Estelle Wyss."

The memory still brought Sara pain. "How is she?"

"She was fine. Her husband . . . Kyle . . ."

"Karl."

"Karl. He passed away."

"I know. I sent a condolence card. I knew Estelle wouldn't take my call. Where did you see her?"

"I went to their home. Actually, I'm still parked in front of it."

"Why?"

"Just . . ." Something stopped him. "Business."

"Business?" Sara asked. "Hadn't you done enough 'business' with the Wysses?"

Stupid thing to say, he thought. *Other than that, Mrs. Lincoln, how was the play?* "So, you called about Le Jardin?"

"In part. Steve tells me that you haven't signed the divorce papers yet."

"No, I haven't."

"May I ask why?"

"I've had second thoughts."

"Don't tell me you're not happy with the settlement." An edge of anger had crept into her voice.

"No. I'm just . . ." he hesitated. What he had intended to say now seemed absurd even to himself.

"You're just what?"

"I'm not sure I want it to end."

"Want what to end?"

"Us. Our marriage."

There was a long pause. "Are you kidding?" she finally asked, her voice rising.

"No."

"'Us' has been over a long time, Jim. And it's not your choice anymore." Sara sighed. "Isn't it really because I looked worse than you thought and you've decided to wait for me to die so you can take everything?"

"No, Sara, I would never . . ."

"Of course you wouldn't," she said. "Just sign the papers, Jim. It's time for this *mistake* to end."

The full force of his own words hit him. "I'm sorry I said that."

"Me too. More than you will ever know. Goodbye, Jim." She hung up.

Kier flipped his phone shut. *This just keeps getting better.*

CHAPTER

Twenty-seven

When Linda came that afternoon the house was dark and appeared vacant. The kitchen counter was covered with white Chinese takeout boxes.

"Mr. Kier?"

Kier's voice came from above. "In my room."

Linda climbed the stairs. The bedroom light was off and the blinds drawn. Kier was lying on top of the covers looking at the ceiling. "Are you okay?"

"No one punched me out today, if that's what you're asking."

"I was. May I turn on the light?"

"Sure."

She switched the light on. Kier shielded his eyes with his hand. "I left the papers you brought on the kitchen table," he said. "They're all signed."

"Thanks. How did your meeting with Mrs. Wyss go?"

"I don't know."

"Well, she didn't punch you."

"I wish she had. It wouldn't have hurt as much."

Linda leaned back against the wall. "What did she do?"

"She forgave me. She forgave me for taking away her dreams, her life, and her faith in the human race. And she wasn't trying to be spiteful. She meant it. Where do I go with that?"

Linda shrugged. "I don't know what to tell you."

"Two down and I've accomplished nothing." He combed his fingers through his hair. "Sara called me. First time in . . . I don't know how long. Forever. Do you know how I felt when I saw her name on my phone?"

Linda shook her head.

"I felt like I'd come home."

"Why did she call?"

"She wanted to know why I haven't signed the divorce papers. I told her I wasn't sure I wanted to end our marriage."

"What did she say to that?"

"She said it was over a long time ago." He sighed.

Linda looked down. "I'm sorry."

"Something good has to come from this, doesn't it?"

"I hope so. Do you need anything?"

"No," he said softly. "Thanks for coming by."

"You're welcome." She turned to go. "Do you want the light off?"

"Please."

She switched off the light. "See you tomorrow."

"Tomorrow," Kier said. "There's always tomorrow."

CHAPTER

Twenty-eight

It was nearly ten o'clock, and Sara was getting ready for bed when her phone rang. She smiled when she saw the name on the caller ID. "Hi, sweetheart. How was your day?"

"I've got a problem," Jimmy said.

Sara's smile fell. "What kind of problem?"

"Juliet wants to have the reception at Le Jardin."

"I know. She told me."

"So what do I do?"

"I don't understand what the problem is. Juliet seemed very happy."

"Oh, she's over the moon. Especially when they told her they'd give us the space at no charge. I just don't get it. When I offered to pay for the reception she got mad."

Sara sighed. "It's not the same thing," she said. "We own Le Jardin, so getting it free doesn't feel like she's insulting her parents by suggesting they can't afford it. Jimmy, Le Jardin's a beautiful place. It doesn't matter where your wedding is, it just matters that you two are together."

"I don't want *him* at my wedding," he blurted out.

"Him? You mean your father?"

"Yes, my father. Juliet thinks not inviting him is a mistake. Especially now since we're having it at Le Jardin." He exhaled in exasperation, then said more calmly, "What do you think?"

"It doesn't matter what I think."

"It matters to me."

"If you really want to know, Jimmy, I agree with Juliet."

Jimmy didn't respond.

"I know it's hard between you and your father, but this is a chance to mend things."

"I don't get it, Mom. After all he's done

to you, why do you still defend him? Why can't we just move on?"

Sara's voice softened. "Because in spite of all that's happened, a part of me still loves him."

Jimmy was stunned. "How could you still love him?"

"Because I choose to. And I choose to because I know him. I know who he really is, even if he's forgotten." Sara lay back on her bed and sighed. "I wish we could have this conversation in person, Jimmy. All you know of your father is a profit-obsessed, ruthless businessman who was never there for you. But he wasn't always that way.

"We were poor as church mice when we got married. But we were in love and we thought we had all we needed. Back then your father was generous to a fault. Once, he overheard me talking to a neighbor after her husband lost his job. He talked me into using what little savings we had to fill their cupboards with groceries. He never turned anyone away. I used to get mad at him about it."

"You got mad at Dad for being *too* generous?"

"Long ago, I did. But he was a good man. And I knew that I'd rather have a good husband than a rich one.

"He was a good father too. He doted over you. He would come home after a hard day at work and you would run to him. He loved that. He'd swing you around and you'd both be laughing. Half the time you wouldn't even come to me. Do you remember any of that?"

Jimmy turned quiet. "I have some memories."

"His dream was to be a guidance counselor for troubled youth. Most people assume your dad was a business major. He wasn't. He has a major in social work. After he graduated he went back for his master's.

"It wasn't easy. We were struggling to make ends meet and pay for college. I was working as a secretary at a law office for twelve hundred a month. Then I got pregnant. We had no idea how we would make it, but we were excited to start our family. We just had faith that things would work out. But then I had complications with the pregnancy and I had to stop working. Back in those days we used to put our money in a pickle jar. I remember one Sunday evening just sitting there looking at that jar and wondering how we were going to eat. I counted it over and over like it would change the amount. I still remember how much was in the jar: twenty-two dollars and seventy-four cents. I was sick and helpless and worried and it was killing your father. He felt so guilty. I'll never forget the night he said, 'It's too much. It's too much.' It was a pivotal moment for all of us.

"He called his father and was on the construction site the next day. He quit school in the middle of the semester. He never went back."

"His father, Grandpa James, was thrilled. He was always unhappy about Dad's choice of career. In fact, when Dad went back for his master's, his father didn't speak to him for nearly six months. It was hard on your dad. Like most sons he wanted to please his father, but Grandpa was pretty clear about how disappointed he was with him."

"Like Dad is with me?"

Sara hesitated. "Yes, like Dad is with you. You have to understand, Jimmy, that sometimes people try to validate their own decisions, good and bad, by enforcing on others what they've imposed on themselves. To support you in your dream would be to admit your father gave up on his own. That's a hard thing for anyone to stomach. It doesn't make it right, but it's true."

Jimmy countered, "If giving up his dream was so painful, then why is Dad so against mine? If anyone should understand it should be him."

"I know, sweetheart, but it just doesn't work that way. Leaving his dream behind wasn't what your father wanted, it's what he believed was right for his family. That's a noble thing. He sacrificed what *he* wanted for *us*. Then you were born and he worked all the harder. He wanted to give us a good life. He wanted me to feel secure. He wanted all of us to have a future. We built a nice little nest egg. We bought our first home." Sara smiled fondly in recollection, her pleasure was reflected in her voice. "It was tiny, but we made it nice, we had a nice little garden in back and tulip beds in front. Those were good days. We would go on long Sunday walks around Sugar House Park pushing you in your stroller. We'd bring stale bread to feed the ducks. We were a family."

Sara's voice fell. "It was about this time that your dad was approached by one of the developers he had been doing work for. This man and a couple lawyers were working on a development and they offered to bring him in. We were excited. We thought we had finally hit the big time.

"I remember listening in when your Dad called his father and told him about the deal. It was the first and only time I ever heard his father say that he was proud of him.

"But what we thought was our big break, wasn't. We thought his new partners were good men. One of them even went to our church. We didn't have the experience to understand that they were really just using us.

"His partners knew it was a risky deal, that's why they brought in Dad. They not only took our nest egg, but they were setting Dad up to take the fall in case things didn't work out. And they didn't. The development failed and his partners left him holding the bag. The creditors came after us. They put liens against our home; they harangued us day and night. His so-called partners made sure that he had signed on everything. While they skipped on to the next deal, we lost everything we had built up, including our home. Those were awful days. Dad was depressed. He started second-guessing everything he did. He asked my advice on the smallest of decisions. It was as if he'd completely lost faith in himself. Those men had broken his spirit.

"But even in those dark days, his goodness prevailed. He tried to do the right thing, the honorable thing. He negotiated payment with all the creditors and slowly paid them off.

"Your father showed his true self in other ways. In the middle of this mess one of his carpenters was diagnosed with multiple sclerosis. Your dad kept him on as long as he could, even when he could barely do his job. Then, when the man couldn't work anymore, Dad hired his wife. He kept her even when we were struggling to get by."

"Linda," Jimmy said.

"That's right," said Sara.

"I've always wondered why she's stuck with him for so long."

I kept telling your dad to go after those

men, to get them to help pay off the debt, but he just said they didn't care. He was right. They wouldn't even take his calls.

"Finally, I think because of my nagging, he went to one of the men's offices and confronted him. The man just laughed him off. He told Dad that he got what he deserved—that only a fool didn't look after himself first and that someday he would thank him for the lesson.

"He told your dad that business had nothing to do with what a man *should* do, only what a man *could* do. And if the weak tree falls, it was so the stronger tree could rise. Eat or be eaten.

"Your father didn't come home that night, nor the next. I remember holding you on the couch, sobbing and praying that he would come home safe. I didn't care about our debt or our house; I just cared about him. You were four, and you kept asking me why I was crying and where Daddy was. I was terrified that something bad had happened to him. Or that he had done something to himself.

"He returned three days later; to this day I don't know where he went. What frightened me the most was that he acted as if *nothing* had happened. But something had. Something profound.

"Your father went back to work with a vengeance. He started working seven days a week, staying late every night. It took him almost three years to pay off the debt those men left us, but he did it. Only when he finished he wasn't the same man. He was stronger and smarter but he was angry."

"I'd be angry too," Jimmy said.

"Anyone would. The problem is, his anger wasn't really about those men. It was about himself. He hated himself for being so trusting and naive and letting them walk all over him. And that's a more dangerous type of anger. It changed the way he saw everything and everyone because it had changed the way he saw himself."

Sara's voice cracked. "Eventually that anger grew strong enough to drive a wedge between us. I should have seen it coming; maybe I did, but I just didn't think it was possible. It's ironic that the thing he did to save our family ended up tearing us apart. But don't forget, your father never intended for it to be this way, Jimmy. That's not who he was."

Jimmy was quiet. "I don't know the man you're describing."

"You still have time to get to know him."

"I'm sorry, Mom, but I think the time's passed."

"No," she said firmly, "it's not over."

"So, if he came back to you right now, would you take him?"

"It depends on which man came back. If it was the man I fell in love with, I would, with all my heart."

CHAPTER

Twenty-nine

David Carnes

Your friend from high school. He came to you in confidence, and you used the information to benefit yourself. (I remember you calling it an "end-around" play.)

Current home address unlisted.

Place of employment: Provanti Building, 670 West 482 South, Orem.

It took Kier nearly a week after his visit with Estelle Wyss before he was ready to approach the next person on his list: David Carnes.

Of the five people on the list, Kier knew Carnes the best. They had been friends through much of middle and high school and had even spent graduation night together, party hopping and cruising State Street in Carnes's silver Pontiac Firebird. It wasn't until a year after high school when Carnes left for Oregon State that the two of them lost contact. Twelve years later

Carnes returned to Utah, a successful financial advisor.

Carnes had united with a group of investors who were planning on developing a golf course community in the south end of the Salt Lake valley. They had completed most of the preliminary work but had yet to secure a particular piece of property vital to the development. Carnes learned that the owner of the property, MAC management, was a business associate of Kier's so he went to Kier for some friendly advice on how to negotiate the deal. Because of the still unresolved nature of the project, Carnes was operating under strict confidentiality agreements with his development partners that required him to have Kier sign a non-disclosure agreement before sharing with him their plans; but because they were old friends Carnes ignored the formality.

Kier was impressed with the project and told Carnes that he'd see what he could do to help. As soon as Carnes left his office Kier contacted his associate at MAC and purchased the property himself. He doubled the property's price, then went directly to Carnes's partners and forced himself into the project. The partners, angry with Carnes for disclosing confidential information that cost them a substantial amount of money and equity, kicked him out of the deal and Kier took his place as a majority share-holder. The project was as successful as the group anticipated and netted Kier millions. Carnes never confronted Kier about the betrayal. He hadn't seen or heard from Carnes since that meeting in his office.

✳

The address on the memo led Kier to a modern seven-story building on the out-skirts of Orem. It was the only building above two stories for miles. Kier parked in a thirty-minute visitors parking stall out front and walked up the concrete stairs to the building.

The interior of the building was as im-pressive as the exterior, a glass atrium that was the height of the building. The lobby was bright and spacious; on one wall hung a vinyl banner with a bottle of juice nearly sixty feet tall. The floor was black marble.

A kidney-shaped stainless steel and glass receptionist station stood in the center of the lobby, vibrant red poinsettia plants surrounding its base. Two attractive blond young women wearing headsets were busily answering calls. Behind the women, in gold, three-foot-tall letters mounted on backlit, frosted glass was the word P R O V A N T I.

As Kier approached the desk one of the young women looked up at him and smiled. "May I help you?"

"I'm here to see David Carnes."

"Do you have an appointment?"

"No. I just thought I'd drop by."

She gave him a peculiar look. "I'll have to call his office. Your name?"

"James Kier. Mr. Carnes and I are old friends," he said, thinking he should have emphasized the word "old" more than "friends."

"Thank you. Just a moment, please."

She pushed a button on the phone console and spoke into her headset, "Shantel, there's a Mr. James Kier to see Mr. Carnes. James Kier. That's right. No, he doesn't have an appointment. He said they're old friends. Okay."

She looked back at Kier. "She'll see if Mr. Carnes is available. He's on the phone right now so it will be a few minutes. Let me have you sign in first, then please have a seat."

Kier signed his name on the ledger. "Is this building all Provanti?"

"Yes, sir."

"What exactly is Provanti?"

"We're an online nutritional company. Provanti juice is our flagship product. It's a super-juice made from the Brazilian mochanut."

"What does it do?"

"Provanti enhances well-being, promotes weight loss, and boosts energy. I've even had people tell me it cures cancer."

"Maybe I should get a bottle."

"You should," she said proudly. "We sell more than a half billion dollars of Provanti a year."

Kier looked at her incredulously. "A half *billion* dollars?"

"That was last year. We expect to exceed that this year. And last October we introduced a line of skin care products using the mochanut."

Kier shook his head. "A half billion dollars. I'm in the wrong business. So what does Mr. Carnes do here?"

The woman smiled. "Mr. Carnes is the founder and CEO of Provanti. Excuse me." She pushed a button. "Yes. Thanks,

Shantel." She reached under her desk and pulled out a plastic tag printed with the word VISITOR. "Mr. Carnes will see you. Here's your visitor's pass. Take the elevator to the seventh floor. Shantel will meet you and take you back."

"Carnes is the founder," Kier said.

"Yes he is."

Kier took the pass, clipping it to his front pocket. "Thank you."

"You're very welcome. The elevators are to your left."

Kier walked over to the double elevators and pushed the up button. One of the elevators immediately opened. He stepped inside and pushed seven. The interior of the elevator was all mirrors except for a plexiglass poster with a picture of a beautiful woman jogging on the beach and copy expounding on the virtues of Provanti. A moment later the door opened to a lobby panelled in dark wood and hung with lush oil paintings. There were two couches facing each other and each was upholstered in tucked bomber jacket leather with carved pineapple feet. A beautiful woman in an elegantly tailored gray suit, and lavender silk blouse approached him. "Mr. Kier? This way please."

She led him around the corner to a single door. "Mr. Carnes is in his office. He's expecting you."

"Thank you." He unclipped the visitor's tag and shoved it into his pants pocket, then stepped through the door.

The office was huge. Near the back was an oversized walnut desk framed by an enormous mural depicting an exotic jungle scene. The wood blinds were all drawn and the lighting was indirect, creating a particularly rich ambience. Carnes, a handsome, athletically built man, sat in the middle of it all in a forest green tucked-leather chair that looked more throne than office furniture.

"James Kier." He motioned to the three leather chairs in front of the desk. "Have a seat."

Kier sat down in the middle chair. "Nice office."

"Thank you. I designed it myself. Those bookshelves there are made of Makore wood, imported from Ghana. I had them made for my collection of first editions." He stood and walked over to the bookshelves, which ran nearly the entire length of the wall and pulled out a book. "This is my prize, *Gone with the Wind,* signed by Margaret Mitchell. I also have six Steinbecks, signed of course, and *A Christmas Carol* signed by Dickens. I won't tell you how much that cost me, unless you ask."

"Impressive," Kier said, as surprised by Carnes's good humor as his hubris. "So, you've done well since I last saw you."

Carnes walked back over to his desk. "Business has been *good.*"

"And the family? How's Heather?"

"We dissolved that partnership about three years ago."

"I'm sorry to hear that."

"No need. People change. We're on better terms now than when we were married." He leaned back. "I'm surprised to see you."

"Because of our parting?"

"Actually, because I thought you were dead. I read about it in the *Tribune.*"

"The newspaper got it wrong."

"That's too bad," Carnes said.

Kier smiled. "That I'm not dead or that the newspaper got it wrong?"

Carnes smiled back wryly. "Pick one." He leaned back in his chair. "You should know it brought me no small satisfaction to learn of your death."

"You must be very disappointed."

"I'll get over it. So what brings you to my kingdom?"

"I came to tell you I'm sorry."

"Sorry for what?"

"You know what."

"Yes, but I want to know that you do. I want to hear it from your own slippery tongue."

"Fair enough. I took the information you trusted me with and used it for my own profit."

Carnes nodded. "That pretty much sums it up. Are you dying?"

"No."

Carnes looked Kier over, sizing him up. "So, exactly what kind of 'sorry' do you mean?"

"I don't understand the question."

"Are you 'sorry you're a thief,' 'sorry you're the kind of guy who would steal from a friend,' or 'sorry' your actions have finally caught up to you and you need something from me, so you've come to apologize."

Kier thought it over. "The first two."

"Good. Though I was hoping it was the third. It would have been blissfully poetic to have you need my help."

"I bet."

"So let me tell you what I think of you and your apology," Carnes said, his face lit with an arrogant smile. "I think you're a worm, Kier. A parasite and blight on humanity." He lifted both hands. "There you are. So now that you know what I think of you are you still sorry?"

Kier looked down for a moment. "If I had to do it over again, I would do things differently."

Carnes nodded. "Not bad. I almost believe you."

"Why wouldn't you believe me?"

"Because, leopards don't change their spots."

"Not usually."

Carnes's eyes flashed with sudden passion. "I don't know what really brought you here, Kier. Maybe you found religion or cancer or maybe even a conscience, but frankly it doesn't matter to me. Your 'sorry' serves only you. You're wasting my time."

Kier stood. "Then I'm also sorry for wasting your time."

Carnes threw back his head and laughed. "Sit down, I'm just punking you. I'm genuinely intrigued by this visit." He leaned forward. "See this watch? It's a Patek Philipe. They call it the million-dollar watch. It makes a Rolex look like a Timex. You know why I'm telling you this?"

"Either you think I'm interested in timepieces or you want me to know how rich you are."

Carnes laughed. "Haven't lost that sense of humor, have you? Actually, you're right. I want you to know how rich I am so that you can fully appreciate the irony of this situation."

"Which is?"

"That everything you see around you, everything I am, is, in part, because of you."

The revelation brought Kier no pleasure. "Explain."

"That little fiasco with you—and in the grand scheme of things it truly was little— was devastating for me at the time. But it was exactly what I needed. You gave me two gifts of wisdom that have influenced everything I've done since. First, you taught me to trust no one. Everyone is looking out for themselves, so you better do the same.

"Eat or be eaten." Kier mumbled, as if conjuring up a spirit from the past.

"That's right. Second, winners don't follow everyone else's rules. There are no 'shoulds' or 'oughts' or even right or wrong in business, only what you can get away with and what you can't, nothing more. A lion doesn't give its prey fair warning before it pounces. It doesn't search out the strongest or fastest impala to even the odds; it searches for the weakest, then feeds. It's survival instinct. The greater the mismatch, the better the feast. I took that lesson into the business world and it's rewarded me well. In fact, I'm writing a book about it. It's called *Predator or Prey*. Great title, eh? I've already got a publisher and my publicist tells me I've got a shot at Larry King and *GMA*."

Kier was speechless.

"Oh, and there's a third gift you indirectly gave me. I decided that if being in the real estate development business meant working with people like you, I'd do something else. So I tried my hand at a few things—

seminars, infomercials, MLMs. I eventually found my niche in Internet marketing, selling exotic fruit juices at two dollars an ounce. So, again thanks to you, here I am. I own a mansion in Alpine, a ski condo in Vail, an apartment in Manhattan, a bungalow on Catalina, and a little summer home in Chianti surrounded by vineyards. My home in Alpine has a custom garage for my seventeen cars, including my Lamborghini, a '39 Rolls Silver Shadow, and a Bugatti Veyron." His eyebrows rose. "Now there's a car for you."

"Isn't a Veyron a million dollars?" Kier asked.

"A million euro and worth every penny. She tops out at 407 kilometers; that's 253 miles per hour. At full throttle she'll burn out her tires in fifteen minutes."

"*Practical*," Kier said.

Carnes laughed. "A far cry from that Pontiac Firebird we used to tool around in."

Kier nodded. "A far cry."

"I also have a seventy-foot yacht at the Balboa Beach Yacht Club, a private jet, and I own this building outright. You know I don't know if I should kiss you or punch you."

"You've done well for yourself," Kier said again. "How are your children?"

Carne's expression darkened. "They do their thing. Andy's a ski bum, Clara's in drug rehab, and Marci, I honestly don't know. She's in Europe somewhere. We don't talk anymore."

Kier nodded. "Jimmy and I haven't talked for a while."

Carnes shrugged. "They make their choices. You give them everything and they hate you for it. Go figure."

"Our paths are more similar than you know," Kier said. "For which I am truly sorry." He stood. "Sorry to waste your time."

"No problem, Kier. I've enjoyed our conversation. You sure you're not dying?"

"Not that I know of."

"Then maybe we should get together for a drink sometime. Speaking of which, you should try some Provanti. Even if you're not dying, it could do you good."

"I will. Good luck with your book."

"I'll send you a first edition when it comes off press." He buzzed his assistant. "Show Jimmy the way out and fix him up with some juice and swag."

Shantel appeared at the door. "This way, Mr. Kier. I have some things for you at my desk."

"Parting gifts," Carnes said. He stood and extended his hand. "Really, Jimmy-boy, call me sometime. We predators need to stick together." Kier shook Carnes's hand and followed the young woman out the door.

Shantel loaded him up with a box of juice, a Provanti sweatshirt, pen set, and a vinyl Provanti bag to carry it all.

Back in his car he took a bottle of juice from the carton and held it up to the light. "Provanti. The official drink of predators everywhere."

CHAPTER

Thirty

When Linda stopped at Kier's house on her way home she found him in his kitchen eating a bowl of breakfast cereal. Next to his bowl was a glass of purple Provanti juice.

"Cap'n Crunch. I see you've strayed from your usual diet." She walked around the table. "I brought the Gold's Gym lease on the Holladay shopping center. They want a three-year contract with an additional three-year option, the annual bump not to exceed a dollar a square foot. Basically what you agreed to last week."

"Just leave it; I still want to look it over."

She set it on the table. "So how did things go today?"

He took another bite of cereal. "I went and saw David Carnes."

"And?"

"He has a company called Provanti. It's worth more than a billion dollars."

"Wow. I didn't know it was that big. My sister drinks Provanti every morning. She says it helps her lose weight."

"Carnes *owns* the company. And the building."

"I know."

"You knew?"

She nodded.

"I guess I'm the only one who didn't."

"I'm glad he's done well for himself. So your meeting went okay?"

"It was the worst yet. Carnes sat there throwing out the same Machiavellian excuses I've used for years, and credited me for teaching them to him. It was like having a serial killer thank you for selling him weapons. He's even writing a book about it— *Predator or Prey.* I've created a monster." Kier took a drink of the juice then puckered. "This is awful."

"I know. I've tried it. Tastes like goat sweat."

Kier looked at her, stifling a laugh. "Goat sweat?" She nodded. Kier took his glass and bowl over to the sink and rinsed them out. "Have you had any luck finding Celeste Hatt?"

"Not yet. But I haven't given up."

He walked back to the table. "Then just one more to go. Gary Rossi. Anything special I should be warned about?"

Linda was hesitant. "Yes, but I don't think I should tell you."

"Why is that?"

"It would probably be best for you to find out for yourself."

"That sounds ominous." He lifted the documents and looked them over. "Got a pen?"

"Here."

He signed the lease, then handed it back to Linda.

"When are you going to see Rossi?" Linda asked.

"When I get back."

"Back? You're going somewhere?"

"I need you to book a flight for me to Boston."

Linda smiled. "Are you going to see Jimmy?"

"I'm going to try."

"When would you like to leave?" She took out her PDA.

"As soon as I can."

"Very well. I'll text you the flight info."

"Thank you."

Linda went to the front door, then turned back. "Jimmy will be so happy to see you."

"I hope so," Kier said. In his heart, he knew otherwise.

CHAPTER

Thirty-one

The last time Kier had spoken to his son was more than six months earlier when Jimmy had called to tell him that Sara had cancer. Kier's response was less than sympathetic—not that he didn't care, rather that he was stunned. Jimmy wasn't pleased. His final words to his father—before slamming down the phone—still resonated with him: "You should be the one dying."

Kier's flight landed at Logan International around two in the afternoon. He checked into a hotel near the airport, then took a cab to the Massachusetts College of Art and Design.

Kier went to the housing office and located his son's dorm. He was knocking on the door when a passing student told him that Jimmy was still in class but should return before long. Kier sat in the student lounge for more than an hour, waiting.

Jimmy arrived back around five, a backpack over one shoulder. He froze when he saw his father. He looked more angry than surprised. "What are you doing here?"

"I came to see you," Kier said calmly.

Jimmy walked past him. "A phone call wouldn't suffice?" Kier got up from his chair and followed him down the hall. Jimmy unlocked the door to his room and walked inside.

Kier followed him in uninvited. "I was hoping that maybe I could take you out to dinner."

Jimmy emptied his backpack. "I'm meeting with my study group tonight. I have a final tomorrow."

"You've got to eat."

He looked up at his father. "We haven't spoken for months. What did you expect?"

"I thought," Kier stopped to correct himself, "I had *hoped* that maybe if I flew out here you might give me a chance."

"A chance for what?"

"To apologize. And to fix things between us. Or at least start."

Jimmy looked down for a moment. "Look, I appreciate you making the time to drop by, but this isn't going to happen. As far as I'm concerned, there's nothing between us and there never will be."

Kier frowned. "I'm sorry to hear that." He took a deep breath and looked around the room; the bed was unmade and a pile of dirty clothes sat in a corner. An art portfolio leaned against the wall. "This isn't bad."

Jimmy put his hands in his pockets, *clearly* annoyed that his father wasn't leaving. Kier looked at the oil painting hanging above Jimmy's desk. "Is that Juliet?"

"Yes."

"It's beautiful. The girl *and* the portrait. You're very talented."

"That's the first time you've ever said anything about my paintings. Or my girl."

"Jimmy, I've done, or not done, a lot of things I'm not proud of." He stepped away from the desk. "Anyway, it sounds like you've made up your mind. So I'll leave."

"Don't you have other business out here?" He sounded surprised.

"No, I came to see you. But you're right. I should have called first." Kier looked into his son's eyes. "I know you don't like me, Jimmy. I understand that. I didn't like my father either. I didn't even go to his funeral. When I was younger I planned on being a different kind of father to you, but obviously I failed. I regret not going to my father's funeral. But not as much as I regret not being the father you needed."

Just then Jimmy's roommate walked in.

"Hey, Jimmy, some old dude was . . ." He stopped when he saw Kier:

"Give us a minute," Jimmy said.

"No worries." He walked out. Kier watched him leave then turned back to Jimmy. "If you ever need anything, just call. I may be twenty years too late, but at this point, it's all I can do."

Jimmy said nothing.

"Take care of yourself." Kier walked toward the door. Then he looked back and their eyes met. "I hope you can find a way to forgive me someday." He turned and walked out.

As he left the building he felt an overwhelming grief. There was a time when his son ran to him. Now Jimmy couldn't wait until he was gone. *What I wouldn't give for a second chance,* he thought as he hailed a taxi.

CHAPTER

Thirty-two

It had been more than nine years since Linda's husband, Max, had been diagnosed with multiple sclerosis. It had progressed relatively slowly manifesting itself mostly in numbness and general weakness, until six years later when he was confined to a wheelchair and the disease had progressed more rapidly. For nearly two and a half years Linda had taken her lunch break at home so she could take care of her husband. It was noon and she was about to leave the office when the phone rang. "Kier Company. Linda Nash speaking."

"Linda? It's Sara."

Linda smiled. "Sara, it's so good to hear from you." When she first started working for James Kier, she spoke with Sara nearly every day, but it had been a long time since Sara had called the office. "How are you doing?"

"I'm still here, thank you. And how is Max?"

She sighed a little. "Not so well. He had another MRI last week. They found three more lesions on his spinal cord."

"Tell him he's in my prayers."

"Thank you, I will. And you're in our prayers, Sara. Are you calling for Mr. Kier? Because he's not in right now."

"Actually, I'm calling to talk to you. I need to know what's going on with Jim."

"What do you mean?"

"He's acting peculiarly. Last week he told me that he doesn't want to sign the divorce papers, then yesterday he flew to Boston to see Jimmy. He even tried to make amends to a former friend of mine he was in business with years ago."

"Estelle Wyss?"

"Yes. You knew?"

"Mr. Kier's been trying to make amends with a number of people."

"Amends? Why?"

"It started with that obituary. He was pretty shaken up by what he read in the online comments. He decided he wanted to change."

Sara thought this over. "Change himself or change what they thought of him?"

"I don't know."

"Will you let me know when you do? It's very important."

"Yes. I promise."

"Thank you, Linda. And if you don't mind, I'd prefer that Jim not know that I called."

"I understand. And it's good to hear from you. Take care of yourself."

"You too. Give Max and Mason my love."

Linda slowly returned the phone to its cradle, thinking how much she missed Sara's calls. She thought over Sara's question. Was he trying to change himself or just what people thought of him. She wondered if her boss even knew the answer himself.

CHAPTER

Thirty-three

Kier was sitting near his flight's gate, waiting for his flight to board, when his phone rang. It was the sixth time that Lincoln had called since he'd arrived in Boston.

"Hey, Lincoln."

"Where have you been?" He sounded exasperated. "I've been trying to reach you for days."

"Actually, only a day and a half. Boston."

"What are you doing in Boston?"

"I came to see Jimmy."

Lincoln sounded a little calmer. "How did it go?"

"As well as I should have expected. So why are you hunting for me?"

"The divorce papers are due tomorrow. Yesterday I got a message from Sara's attorney. He says if they're not signed by tomorrow they'll consider our agreement void and they're going back for half of Kier Company."

Kier thought it over. "Okay."

There was a long pause "Okay? Okay what?"

"Okay let him go for it."

"Don't get nuts on me here, Jim. Sara has a better than even chance of winning this in court. You could lose half your company."

"I don't think it will happen."

"I'm not saying it will, but why take the chance? Just sign the papers and let's put this behind us. When do you get back?"

"I'm boarding my flight right now."

"Great," he said, relieved. "I'll meet you at the airport."

"You're not listening to me, Lincoln. I'm not signing the papers."

"Jim, you don't understand how serious the situation is. We're talking millions of dollars."

"I understand precisely how serious this is, Lincoln. The company is half Sara's anyway. She's only getting what she deserves."

"Listen to yourself! You've become your own worst enemy."

"You're right about that. I'll call when I'm back."

"No, wait—"

Kier flipped his phone shut then slid it in his carry-on and boarded the flight.

CHAPTER

Thirty-four

By the time Kier landed he knew exactly where he was going, or at least who he wanted to see. He just didn't know where to find him. As soon as the plane taxied to the gate, he turned on his phone and called Linda.

"Are you back?" she asked.

"Just landed. I need you to call Dr. Kuo, get the name of Sara's oncologist, then call me back."

"I'll get right on it. How'd everything go with Jimmy?"

"About the same as the rest of my visits."

Linda sighed. "I'm sorry. I'll text you the info as soon as I have it."

By the time Kier reached his car he had the doctor's name and address. He threw his bag in the back seat and drove to the Huntsman Cancer Center.

He walked up to the reception desk, glancing down at his cell phone to make sure he got the name right. A maternal-looking woman with gray hair smiled pleasantly at him. "May I help you?"

"I'm looking for Dr. Halestrom."

"Dr. Halestrom's on the third floor. Room 312."

"Thank you."

Dr. Halestrom's office waiting room was about a third full, and half the room's occupants wore hats or headscarves to conceal their baldness. The young woman sitting behind the desk glanced up as Kier entered. "Yes?"

"Hi. James Kier to see Dr. Halestrom."

"Just go ahead and sign in with the pen right there." She reached for a clipboard. "Is this your first visit?"

"It's not really a visit. I mean, I don't have an appointment. I just need to speak with the doctor about my wife."

The young woman looked at him as if he belonged in the psych ward instead of oncology. "You don't have an appointment?"

"I just need a minute of the doctor's time. My wife is one of his patients. Sara Kier."

Immediately the woman's face lit with recognition. "Of course. Mrs. Kier's a lovely woman. You said you're her husband?"

"I know this is unconventional but I just need a minute of Dr. Halestrom's time. It's very important."

She looked at him doubtfully. "I'll see if Dr. Halestrom can fit you in." She disappeared through an opening behind her. Kier looked over the signs the woman had posted in her workstation.

Life isn't about how to survive the storm but how to dance in the rain.

When life is more than you can stand, kneel.

What if the Hokey Pokey really is what it's all about?

A moment later, she reappeared. "Dr. Halestrom says to take a seat, he'll be with you as soon as he can."

"Thank you."

Kier sat down in the corner of the room near a large ficus plant that draped over several chairs, ensuring his solitude. He lifted a copy of *Newsweek* from the table next to him and began thumbing through it. About ten minutes later a nurse wearing a green smock came through the office door, her eyes scanning the waiting room.

"Mr. Kier?" she said loudly toward the center of the room.

Kier stood. "I'm James Kier."

"This way, please." She held the door for him, then led him down a long coridor to an examination room. She stepped inside, holding the door for him.

"You're here to see Dr. Halestrom?"

"That's right."

"Have a seat. The doctor will be with you shortly."

"Thank you."

Kier sat on a chair in the corner; it was another ten minutes before the doctor came in. He wore a white smock and carried a clipboard. "Hi, I'm Dr. Halestrom. You're Sara's husband?"

"Yes, James Kier." Kier reached out his hand. The doctor gave him a brief, disinterested shake. "What can I do for you, Mr. Kier?"

"I want to know how Sara is."

The doctor looked at him quizzically. "Why don't you ask her?"

"Let's say we're having a little trouble communicating lately. I asume you know we're separated."

"You really should ask Sara. There are privacy laws that prevent my sharing her medical information without her permission. If she wants you to know, I'm sure she'd tell you."

"She doesn't want to talk to me," Kier said flatly. "I know I'm putting you in an awkward position, but I'm not asking for me. I want to help her . . ."

For several moments the doctor just looked at him. Then he shook his head and sighed. "I really shouldn't be doing this, but I'm going to bend the rules because I believe you're acting in her best interest." He took a deep breath and slowly exhaled. "She's dying."

The directness of the doctor's reply hit him. "Dying? Aren't the treatments helping?"

"The treatments are palliative, not curative. That means they're for improving her quality of life *and* prolonging her life. In this regard, the radiation and chemotherapy have been somewhat helpful, but the cancer has continued to spread."

"Does she know this?"

"Of course."

"There's got to be more we can do." Kier tried to keep a note of desperation out of his voice.

"We're doing everything we can."

"What about a pancreas transplant? Money's no object."

"It's not about money. Her cancer has spread through her entire lymph system; there are tumors in her liver, kidneys, lungs, and peritoneum." The doctor leaned back against the counter. "I know it's hard to accept. But you're coming to this a bit late."

Kier combed his hand through his hair. "How long does she have?"

The doctor shrugged. "Only God knows.

She's a strong woman. If it were anyone else I'd give her a few weeks. She could even make a month, but I'd be surprised if it were much longer. She's holding on until your son's wedding."

Kier felt numb.

The doctor looked at Kier. "Anything else?" he asked, not without sympathy.

He shook his head. "She's had to go through all this alone."

"She's had her sister, and her son."

The lump in Kier's stomach now lodged in his throat. "I am so sorry."

"You should tell her that." He walked out of the room. Kier's legs felt wobbly. He sat back down in the chair. *A few weeks?* Things were moving too slowly. Everything, but the cancer.

His legs still felt weak as he walked out to his car. While he drove from the parking lot his phone rang. It was Lincoln. *The man's relentless*, Kier thought. Kier answered, and without waiting for Lincoln to speak, he said, "Here's one for you, old man. The devil visited a lawyer's office and made him an offer. 'I'll increase your income tenfold, give you four months of vacation each year, and you'll live to be a hundred but never look or feel a day over thirty. All I require in return is your wife's soul to rot in hell for eternity.' The lawyer thought about it, then said, 'What's the catch?'"

Kier hung up before Lincoln could speak, shut off his phone, then headed off to see Sara.

CHAPTER

Thirty-five

What was once a daily occurrence now felt remarkably unnatural. Kier hadn't been home, to *Sara's* home, for seven months. The last time he'd been there they hadn't even spoken. He had grabbed the last few boxes of his belongings and walked out as she silently watched him go. He remembered seeing her furtively brush a tear from her cheek. Now he wished they had said something to each other, even if she had only yelled at him. It would have been better than nothing.

It was twilight and the old neighborhood was lit by Victorian-style street lamps, wrapped with strands of twinkling white lights. The bases of many of the lamps were covered in snowbanks as tall as picket fences. In an unspoken annual competition, homes on the street were brightly lit with elaborately designed Christmas decorations.

He was glad to see that there was no car in the driveway; Beth would certainly try to keep him away. He pulled into the driveway and walked up to the front door. He was about to let himself in but stopped; he felt like a door-to-door salesman approaching a house with a *No Solicitors* sign. Instead he rang the doorbell. It was a few minutes before Sara opened the door; it was dark inside but he could still see her clearly enough to read the surprise on her face, as well as her weariness. She just stared at him. Kier was the first to speak. "Can we talk?"

"No." She began to shut the door but he put his hand out and stopped it.

"Sara, please."

"What do you want from me?"

"I just want to talk."

"About what?"

"About us."

"There is no *us*, Jim. Please let go of my door." She tried to push the door closed but wasn't strong enough.

"I need to tell you how sorry I am."

"Why, because I'm dying? So you can divorce me with a clear conscience?"

"No. Because I love you."

Sara began crying. "Don't say that. You can't say that now."

"It's true."

"Why did you go to my doctor? My life is none of your business."

"I had to know how you really were."

"My death isn't any of your business either."

Kier couldn't answer.

"So now you know," she said, her voice trembling. "Please let go of my door." He took his hand away. She pushed the door shut and dead-bolted it.

He shouted through the door. "Sara, I know you love me."

"No, I don't," she shouted back.

"I saw what you wrote next to my obituary."

Sara didn't reply.

"You're the only woman I've ever loved. You're the only woman who has ever loved me. I was a fool to leave you."

Suddenly, the deadbolt slid and the door opened. Sara's expression was fierce. "I loved you, Jim. I loved you with all my heart. And you left me. You left me when I needed you the most. It's too late; it's too late. You can't come back."

She pushed the door shut again and the deadbolt locked. A door across the street opened; someone looked out, then shut the door again. Kier began to cry. "I want to come home, Sara. I know I don't deserve you. I know I can't fix things. But I would if I could. I would give anything to have you back." He pressed his forehead against the door. "I'm so sorry, Sara. I'm so sorry."

Kier fell to his knees. "I'm so sorry." After a few minutes he stood and walked back to his car. Inside the house Sara slumped down against the door and cried.

CHAPTER

Thirty-six

Gary Rossi

You started Rossi's restaurant with Gary, then forced him out of the business a year later. His last known residence was 924 East 1355 South Magna, Utah. Phone number unlisted.

Kier woke the next morning with Sara's words echoing in his memory. "You left me when I needed you the most. It's too late; it's too late."

✦

Throughout his life Kier had always been good at fixing things. When he was thirteen the gas-powered lawn mower broke halfway through a cutting. While his father called Sears to yell at the clerk who sold them the machine, Kier tore apart the Briggs & Stratton engine. He dissected the block, pulled out the valves, and scraped the ash from the piston. When he put it all back together it ran.

Relationships were something else. Long ago, in college, he thought he was good with people, but not anymore. Too many variables. Too many nuances. Too much unpredictability. He once told Brey, "The more I know people the better I like my car."

He had no idea how to fix things with Sara, or even if it were possible. He was like a doctor frantically administering CPR to a patient that wouldn't respond. *When do you call it? When do you just pull up the sheet and pronounce time of death?*

CHAPTER

Thirty-seven

In his state of despair Kier found himself focusing on mundane details. He didn't know where his current path led (from experience, he was thinking nowhere good), he just knew it was somewhere he could put his feet, one step at a time. For now the list was his path. And the path had one more stop.

Most of him longed to quit. He was three for three; technically he had already struck out, but something about what Linda had said about his next visit propelled as well as frightened him. *It would probably be best for you to find out for yourself.* Find out what? He rubbed a hand across his unshaven cheek, then tugged at the lone bandage across the bridge of his nose and pulled it off. His nose was still tender. He hoped Rossi's expected assault would be a verbal one.

It had been more than six years since Kier had met Rossi at a downtown chamber of commerce luncheon. What started with a good meal ended bitterly two years later. Rossi was a victim of the kind of financial maneuvering Kier had once been proud of.

Rossi had come to Kier with an idea for a restaurant, bringing with him a collection of Tuscan family recipes, a roomful of Italian antiques, and a nest egg of $9,000 that he had accumulated over a lifetime of working in other chefs' kitchens. The money was just a fraction of what he'd need to open a restaurant. The two of them quickly reached an agreement: Rossi would provide the ideas, sweat, time, and expertise while Kier provided the bulk of the capital and oversaw the business end of things. The restaurant was called Rossi's, and like most of Kier's ventures, it proved a wild success. Within just a few months of their grand opening they were one of the most talked about restaurants in the city.

A month after toasting their first year in business, Kier decided that he no longer needed Rossi and set about making him redundant. First, Kier persuaded Rossi to hire an ambitious young sous-chef who could run the kitchen so he could "enjoy the fruits of their success." Rossi, dedicated to ensuring the restaurant's success, had worked twelve-to-fourteen-hour days, seven days a week for so long that he heartily thanked Kier for his kindness, never suspecting that he was simply maneuvering him out of the way. Rossi personally trained the new chef and gratefully, took a much needed vacation. Two days after he left, Kier changed the locks on the doors and sent Rossi an e-mail to let him know he was fired and need not return. Not surprisingly, Rossi returned immediately.

Kier offered the desperate Rossi $10,000 for his stock in the restaurant, only a thousand more than Rossi had personally invested and less than 10 percent of the restaurant's monthly profits. Rossi refused. Kier was prepared. He countered with a threat to declare a million-dollar profit without paying out a penny in dividends, putting Rossi in a considerable tax bind.

"You can't use my name," he said.

Kier patted the contract. "I *own* your name."

Flustered, Rossi replied, "Then I'll sell my stock to someone else."

Kier smiled smugly. "That won't be possible." Hidden in the sixty-two-page contract was a clause forbidding Rossi to sell his stock to anyone without the majority stockholder's approval—Kier's approval. In the end it was a choice between taking the deal or personal bankruptcy. He left Kier's office a broken man. As he walked out, Rossi's last words were, "You're a miserable excuse for a human being, Kier. You're a bad man."

"No, I'm just clever. There is no good or bad in business," Kier said, "just smart and . . . you."

Of Kier's many business partings this had been one of the most bitter. Rossi had not only trusted, but admired him. He had even asked Kier to be the godfather to their newborn son; Kier had declined. Fallen heroes hit the ground hardest. Kier hadn't seen or heard from Rossi since that last meeting and wasn't looking forward to this one.

Kier drove to the address Linda had typed on the list. The home was forty minutes away in Magna, Utah, a former copper mining town at the base of the Oquirrh Mountains. Even though the Kennecott Copper mine was still in operation, the town had been in decline for nearly a half century and was now sometimes used by Hollywood directors shooting fifties-era productions.

He arrived at the house shortly after noon, a small bungalow with aluminum siding and green asphalt shingles. There was a mailbox out front with ROSSI spelled out in gold decals.

He climbed out of his car, then walked up to the front porch and knocked on the crimson door.

The door opened; the woman who stood in front of him bore a distinct resemblance to Rossi. Her black hair was streaked with gray and pulled back tightly in a bun. She wore a thick knit sweater accented with a silver crucifix nearly six inches long. Kier had met Rossi's wife and, from what he remembered, was sure this wasn't her. The woman stared at him with disgust, her expression more clear than words could ever be.

"I'm James Kier," he said, pretty sure she already knew.

"I know who you are. What do you want?"

"I'm here to see Gary."

"Gary's not here."

"Will he be back soon?"

"I sincerely doubt it," she said curtly.

"You are . . . ?"

"I'm Gary's sister."

"It's nice to meet you," Kier said, regretting the words even as he spoke them.

She stared at him with an expression that was anything but *nice*. Kier rephrased his earlier question. "Do you know when Gary will be back?"

"The morning of the resurrection."

"Excuse me?"

"Gary's dead." She spoke the words with a certain amount of satisfaction.

Kier blanched. "I'm sorry."

She shook her head, her thin lips pursed tightly together. "So you didn't know. All these years I wondered whether or not you lost sleep over what happened and you didn't even know."

"I don't know what you're talking about."

"Gary went through a real bad time after you swindled him out of his restaurant. He started drinking, lost a half dozen jobs, and then he just went off the deep end. His wife took the kids and left him. I can't say that I fault her, but for Gary it was the last straw. One afternoon he just ended it. Really, I'm surprised you didn't know. Your name was all over his suicide note. In fact, you should read it."

Before he could object she walked away, and came back holding a wrinkled piece of paper. "His last words. Most of them meant for you." She pushed the note into Kier's hands.

Kier tried to hand it back to her. "I really don't want to see this."

"I'm sure you don't, you coward."

Finally, Kier dropped the paper on the ground. Rossi's sister shook her head, stooped and picked it up. "I thought as much. But you're not getting off that easy. If you won't read it, I'll tell you what it said. Gary wrote that he was mixed up in his thoughts of the afterworld, because if there were a God, he wouldn't allow people like you to prosper. But then again, you're the greatest evidence that there is a devil." She read from the note. 'If there be blame, I'll share it with the architect of my destruction, James Kier, may his soul burn for eternity.'"

Kier lowered his head.

"You know, Mr. Kier, I hated you for a long time, a long time. But hate doesn't take you anywhere but down, so I had to let it go. I've even had to accept that Gary's death wasn't your fault. Make no mistake, you're an awful, hell-bound man—but no matter. Gary had a choice to make. He chose to give up.

"I've wondered what I would do if I ever saw you again. I thought I might spit in your face or slap you or heaven knows what. I never imagined you would show up at my own door. But seeing you here, I don't want to do anything but pity you. You are a sad, cankered man. One of the devil's own."

Kier made no effort to defend himself. "You're right."

His humility surprised her. "So you do

have a conscience. I can only imagine what brought you around now. Are you dying?"

"I just wanted to talk to him."

"Why? Got another venture?" she mocked.

"I wanted to apologize. I wanted to see if I could make things right."

"You're a little late for that."

"I'm sorry."

"Yeah, I bet you are." She lifted the note again, taunting him with it. "You're afraid of this, aren't you?" She stepped back and slammed the door. Kier stood there a moment, then turned and walked back to his car.

CHAPTER

Thirty-eight

Linda loved the snow even though it often made her feel melancholy. Tonight, as she drove away from the office, the snow was falling heavily, painting the world around her with its cold indifference. No, her sadness was more than the weather. She was thinking about her boss. She realized, for the first time, how much their relationship had changed in the past few weeks. She truly cared about him, and she was worried about how his final meeting had gone. She wondered if she had done the right thing in not warning him about Rossi's suicide.

She had worked late making preparations for the company's first Christmas party; it was past six o'clock when she arrived at Kier's home. The day had already surrendered to evening, the moonlight reflecting off the front yard's snow.

She rapped on the door then let herself in. The house was dark. "Mr. Kier?" There was no response. She walked to the living room. Kier was there, a shadow in a chair.

"There you are. I brought the Arcadia documents, and Mike had some tax forms you need to sign." She took the papers from her leather portfolio. "He said to tell you, and I quote, 'Not to worry, he's just shifting the tax load to this year.'" She arranged the documents on the glass coffee table and looked up. Kier was looking ahead as if he hadn't heard her. "Mr. Kier?"

Nothing.

"Are you okay?"

"I went to see Gary Rossi." His voice was thin as if stretched close to breaking.

"Oh." She sat down on the couch opposite him, and took off her coat.

"How long have you known?" he asked.

Linda swallowed. "I heard just after it happened."

"Why didn't you tell me?"

"At that point, would you have cared?"

He was silent for a moment. "Probably not." He exhaled loudly. "I went to see Sara last night." His voice cracked. "She's dying."

Linda looked down. "I'm so sorry."

"I told her that I wanted to come home. But she said it's too late."

Tears began to well up in Linda's eyes.

"What a fool I am. When I started all this I actually thought I was being some kind of saint." He laid his head in his hands. "But I'm just a hypocrite. I didn't do it for them, I did it for me and my *legacy*. And I've failed. I've failed everyone. I couldn't make restitution. Not even with myself."

He looked up at her as a tear fell down his cheek. "I don't care about my legacy anymore. I deserved every one of those comments on the Web site and ten thousand more. Those people know the real James Kier." He took a deep breath. "But the worst thing is that now that I really do want to make things better, there's nothing I can do. Maybe this is hell, seeing the truth. Knowing fully the pain and hurt you've caused others and knowing there's no way you can make it better. I've stolen their lives and dreams. I have blood on my hands." He looked into her eyes. "How could I ever be forgiven?"

Linda fought back her tears. "Isn't that the point of Christmas?"

He sighed again, dropping his head in his hands.

"Mr. Kier, you might have started this journey for the wrong reason, but you ended up at the right place. You've changed. It's miraculous how much you've changed. And you've tried to repent. I'm not an expert on forgiveness, but I do know that intent matters. I also know that it's never too late to do the right thing. There are people who still need you and care about you."

"No one cares about me."

"I do."

He looked up at her. "I don't know why. But thank you." Then he asked, "Why did you leave the most important names off the list?"

"I knew if you changed, you would discover that I had. And if you didn't . . ." She paused. "Well, then it really wouldn't have mattered."

Kier began to sob. "They used to love

me. Jimmy and Sara used to love me. I would do anything to have their love again. I would give everything to have a second chance. Everything. But it's too late."

Linda walked over to Kier and put her arms around him. He put his head on her shoulder and wept. At last he composed himself.

"It's late," he said. "You'd better get home to your family."

"What are you going to do?"

"I don't know."

His tone of resignation frightened her. "I'll be back in the morning to check on you." She retrieved her coat and started for the door, then turned around. "Thursday is our first company Christmas party. I don't know if you're planning on attending but you still have a three o'clock meeting with Vance Allen of Scott Homes. Shall I postpone it?"

"No. I'll take the meeting," he said. He dropped his head in his hands.

"I'll see you in the morning." He didn't speak and her heart ached as she looked at him. "Please, Mr. Kier, take care of yourself."

"Goodnight," he said.

*

Linda walked out to her car. It was still snowing heavily and in the short time she'd been inside, her car was already covered. She climbed inside, started the engine and turned the defrost on full, then rooted through her glove box for a travel pack of Kleenex. She wiped her eyes and nose. Then she grabbed the snowbrush from her back seat and climbed out and brushed the snow from her windows. She looked back at the house. It was still dark. "You have changed, Mr. Kier," she said. She climbed back in her car, threw the wet brush on the floor in back, and began to back out of the driveway. Then she remembered her promise. She put her car in park then took out her cell phone and dialed. "Sara, it's me. Linda."

CHAPTER

Thirty-nine

Kier awoke at eight o'clock, the winter sun filling his room with its gold brilliance. Almost immediately he climbed out of bed and began searching through his cupboards and drawers for something he hadn't used for years, something he now felt drawn to. He found his Bible tucked away in a box in the bottom of his closet.

An elderly neighbor, a widow, had given it to him when he was ten years old after he had shoveled her walk for free. He had loved the smell and texture of its leather cover and the beautiful marbled endsheets, and the frontispiece with a woodcut engraving of Mary with her Child. As he grew older he learned to treasure its words.

It had been years since he'd opened the book. Its worn, onion paper pages were well marked with red pencil. Even after all the years he still remembered the passage he was looking for.

Isaiah 1:18. Though your sins be as scarlet they shall be as white as snow; though they be red like crimson, they shall be as wool.

He carried the book over to the window. The evening's snow had blanketed the city in white. Pure white. He wished he could be pure again. To be reborn to a second chance, washed clean from all his mistakes. Linda had said it. *Wasn't that what Christmas was about?*

The doorbell rang. At first he ignored it. He didn't want to see anyone, or anyone to see him. Then he remembered that Linda had promised to come by to check on him. He closed the Bible and set it reverently on his nightstand. The bell rang again, then he heard the door open.

"I'll be right down," he shouted. There

was no reply. He walked out to the mezzanine overlooking the foyer. "Linda?"

It took a moment for his eyes to adjust to the foyer's dim lighting. The woman standing below held a cane and was leaning backward against the door, her cap and shoulders dusted with snow. It was Sara. She looked up at him and their eyes locked in uncertainty. "I let myself in. I hope that's all right."

Kier stared at her. "Sara." He hurried down the stairs. Her gaze never left him. He stopped a few feet from her, wanting to embrace her but afraid to.

"Can we talk?" she asked.

"Of course. Let me get you a chair."

Leaning heavily on her cane she walked toward the living room. Kier took her arm and led her to the couch. He helped her sit, then sat down next to her. Her eyes welled up with tears. "I lied to you. I told you I didn't love you. I do. I'll always love you, Jim. And I miss you."

He threw his arms around her and began to sob. "Oh Sara. I'm so sorry."

She leaned her head on his shoulder and rubbed her hand up and down his back.

"I know you are. I am too. I should have done more."

"You have nothing to be sorry for. It was all me. Can you ever forgive me?"

She leaned back and took his face in her hands so she could look in his eyes. "I already have."

Kier looked at her in wonder. "How could you? I don't deserve it."

"That's what makes it love."

CHAPTER

Forty

CHRISTMAS EVE

Kier Company had never before hosted such an event as their first Christmas bash, and Linda, the party's chief architect, saw to it that it would not be soon forgotten.

The conference room table was covered with a festive red and gold cloth and arrayed with as fine a spread as the season could offer. There were more than two dozen different pastries and sweets: Mexican wedding cookies, pizzelles, raspberry-topped butter cookies, baked meringues, walnut-embedded brownies, miniature éclairs, and chocolate-dipped strawberries.

There were croissants and an assortment of breads and rolls to be made into sandwiches with Swiss, cheddar, provolone, Dubliner, and jalapeño jack cheeses; rare roast beef, smoked turkey, crab salad, honey-baked ham, corn beef, pastrami, and a variety of German and Italian sausages.

Large ice-filled crystal bowls were packed with plump shrimp next to scallop-shaped dishes of cocktail sauce, herring in sour cream and platters of Swedish meatballs and bacon-wrapped scallops.

There were three different kinds of quiches. Sliced bananas, pineapples, apples, mangos, pears, and large seedless red grapes were piled on a silver platter next to cascading fountains of white, milk, and dark chocolates for dipping.

To drink there was hot wassail, soda water with Italian flavorings, and nutmeg-dusted eggnog as thick and rich as melted ice cream.

Christmas music filled the building's hallways. The classics: Burl Ives, Perry Como, and Mitch Miller as well as newer artists like Mariah Carey and Kenny G.

There was a tall Christmas tree in the front lobby, strung with blue lights and silver baubles each with an employees name written in glitter. Someone had hung a sprig of mistletoe above the water cooler, which a few employees had already put to good use.

Kier arrived late and walked around greeting employees, shaking hands and sharing jokes. Kate, from Collections, placed a Santa cap on Kier's head and, to everyone's surprise, he just smiled and made no effort to remove it.

Kier spotted Lincoln at the conference table filling his plate with food. He walked up to him.

"Lincoln, my friend. Merry Christmas."

"Jimmy. Nice bash."

"Thanks for coming."

"Wouldn't have missed it for the world. I figured a party like this might be a once-in-a-lifetime event."

"No, it's going to be an annual event," he said, smiling broadly. "Did you bring the papers?"

"Got them in my car. But why do you want them? I thought you said everything between you and the Missus was copacetic."

"Better than copacetic. Sara and I want to burn them. Kind of a ritual."

"Got it." Lincoln bit into an éclair, the cream erupting from its sides onto his chin.

Linda walked up to the men. "Hi, Lincoln."

"Hi, doll. Merry Christmas."

She grabbed a napkin and dabbed the cream from Lincoln's face. "Hey, I have a Christmas riddle for you. An honest lawyer and Santa Claus were walking together when they both saw a ten-dollar bill on the sidewalk. Which one picked it up?"

Lincoln grinned. "Probably the lawyer."

"No, it was Santa. Everyone knows that honest lawyers don't exist."

Lincoln shook his head. "Et tu, Linda?"

"Sorry."

Kier nodded proudly. "Well done."

Linda smiled and took Kier's arm. "Thank you. Now it's time for your toast. Excuse us, Lincoln."

"Certainly." He went back to the buffet.

Linda led Kier to the center of the office, turned off the music and whistled loudly. "Quiet please. Quiet." The group quieted expectantly. "Mr. Kier would like to share a toast." Linda turned to her boss. "Mr. Kier."

"Thank you."

He looked around the room. In one hand he held a glass of ginger ale and he put his free hand in his pocket. "You know I'm not one for speeches. But if any year deserves one, it's this one. This has been an . . . interesting year. You all experienced my death." There was scattered laughter. "But, more importantly, you've experienced my rebirth. I am grateful for the second chance.

"I hope you all get what you want for Christmas. I got what I wanted. I've spent the last three days with my sweetheart. My wife." He paused. "We humans—at least some of us, are seriously flawed. The things that are the most necessary, the most critical to us, are the things we take most for granted. Air. Water. Love. If you have someone to love, you are lucky. If they love you back, you're blessed. And if you waste the time you have to love them, you're a fool.

"This is my advice to you. Make the most of the time you have with those you love, because . . ." He paused, and for the first time ever the employees of Kier Company saw their boss tear up. ". . . because you don't know when it will end. And the best time to figure that out is ten years ago. But the second best time is right now." He raised his glass. "To second chances."

Everyone raised their glasses. "To second chances."

The noise level rose. Kier lifted his glass again. "One more thing."

Linda whistled again and the place quieted.

"Thank you," Kier said. "To show that I'm serious about what I said—about spending time with your loved ones, I've instructed Tim that we are officially closed between Christmas and New Year's. There will be no business transacted at the Kier Company at this time. You all have the week off with full pay."

The room erupted with wild cheers.

"I wish you all a very Merry Christmas."

There was even more applause and the employees of Kier Company happily crowded around him. Kier smiled and shook hands and as soon as possible stole back to his office. He took off the Santa cap, shut his door, then sat down at his desk. He immediately called home. "Hi, honey."

"How's it going?" Sara asked.

"It's going well. Everyone seems to be having a good time."

"Sorry I couldn't make it. Were they excited about the time off?"

"Ecstatic. How are you feeling?"

"I'm fine. Jimmy and Juliet are visiting."

Kier smiled. "Tell them hello. I've just got this one meeting, then I'll be home."

She didn't say anything.

"Sara?"

"It just sounded so good to hear you say that."

"I love you."

"I love you too." He hung up, and smiled as he lifted the Allen folder. It was much thicker than the last time they'd met; the plans for the new development had been added. As he perused the file's contents there was a knock at his door.

"Come in," Kier said.

Tim Brey poked his head inside. "Got a minute?"

"Sure."

Brey stepped inside carrying a small package. "Linda said you were hiding out back here."

"You know how I am with crowds."

"Well, you wowed this crowd. They were positively giddy."

Kier smiled. "Is anyone still out there?"

"A few of them. But it's finally winding down." He walked up to Kier's desk. "Karen and I have a little Christmas present for you." He held out a package wrapped in gold foil tied with a glossy gold ribbon.

Kier took the present. "Thank you."

"It's just a little something we found at an Amish shop on our vacation back in Bird-in-Hand."

Kier unwrapped the gift. "A music box," he said, "a Christmas music box." He held it up to the lights. It had brass hinges and corners, and a holly leaf flourish was burnished into its polished lid.

"It's beautiful." He opened the lid. Inside was a silver cylinder beneath a glass cover. The cylinder immediately began to turn, plucking from a row of silver tines a Christmas tune: *I heard the bells.* He gently closed the lid and the music stopped. "Thank you. Give Karen and the kids my best."

"I will. Merry Christmas."

"I think that's the first time you've ever said that to me."

"It's the first time I wasn't afraid you would laugh."

"You're probably right. Merry Christmas to you, too. Thanks for all you've done for the company this year."

"It's been my pleasure. So you'll see Sara tonight?"

Kier smiled. "I'm back home. Sara wanted to come today but she didn't feel up to it."

"Well, give her my best. From me and Karen."

"I'll do that."

Brey looked down for a moment then said, "I want to apologize for the things I wrote about you. They were mean, disloyal, and ungrateful."

"Sounds like a good description of me. I'm sorry I ever acted in a way that made you want to write that."

"What you said about second chances, that's true for me as well. Thank you for giving me another chance. I won't let you down."

"I know you won't. I know it."

"I think next year is going to be a very good year for Kier Company."

"I'm sure of that too. Merry Christmas, my friend."

"Merry Christmas, boss. And God bless."

CHAPTER

Forty-one

A few minutes after Brey left his office, Linda's voice came over the speaker. "Mr. Kier, Mr. Allen is here."

"Thank you, Linda. Send him in," he said, then added, "and go on home, it's Christmas Eve."

"I will. I've just a few things to finish up before the very generous holiday you just gave us."

The door opened and Vance Allen stepped hesitatingly into the office, still wearing his overcoat and holding his felt Stetson in his hands.

Kier looked coolly at him from his chair. "Have a seat."

Vance sat down, growing more anxious by the moment.

"So you have my money?"

Vance grimaced. "I have this." He set a check on the desk. "Thirty-seven thousand. It's all I could raise. You can keep it as a bonus. Please, just give me a little more time."

Kier picked up the check. "Where did you get this?"

"I cashed out our 401K, our IRA, everything we had in savings."

"That wasn't wise. The IRS is going to penalize you."

"I know."

He set the check on the desk and pushed it forward. "I'm sorry, I can't take it."

"It's Christmas Eve, Mr. Kier can't you show just a little . . ."

"A little what?"

"Compassion."

Kier took a deep breath. "Compassion, huh. The thing is, if I cut you a break, then what happens? Word gets out that Kier's gone soft. People stop honoring their commitments. Bedlam."

"No one needs to know. It's just between

us. I promise." He leaned forward and pushed the check back. "Please, take the money. I just need a little more time. It's only a month."

Kier took the check and tore it up. "I'm sorry, I'd like to take your money. Really I would. Taking money is one of my favorite things in the world. But I can't."

Vance dropped his head in his hands.

". . . but I can give you more time."

Vance's head rose. "What?"

"I can give you more time."

Vance looked at him incredulously. "How much time?"

"How much do you need?"

"Three weeks. Five tops."

"Okay."

"Okay? Just like that?"

"Just like that. Of course, we'll have to change the terms of our agreement. Adjust the rates a bit."

"How much is a bit?"

"Well, prime is currently 5.7 percent. I'm thinking, say, 6 percent."

"But I'm already paying double that."

"Yeah, you're right. I've overcharged you. How about we just let it ride for the next three weeks. Or five."

Vance's expression changed from wonder to embarrassment. "You're mocking me, aren't you?"

Kier stood, walked around his desk and sat back against its edge. "No, sir. I'm not. Let's just say I've had a change of heart."

Vance looked at him quizzically. Then he asked, "Are you dying?"

Kier laughed. "We're all dying, aren't we? But hopefully not soon."

"I don't know what to say."

"How about 'Merry Christmas.' Now get home to your family." He handed him the pieces of the torn check. "Take this with you. The IRS allows you a fourteen-day window to return the money to your accounts without a penalty. I suggest you do so."

Vance's eyes watered. "God Bless you, Mr. Kier."

"He already has. Merry Christmas."

Vance wiped his eyes, then stood. "It is now." He thrust out his large hand. "Thank you. Thank you very much."

Kier looked at his hand and took it, shaking it firmly. "You're welcome, my friend. I'm sorry for the worry I put you through."

"Forgiven."

After Allen left, Kier shook his head and smiled. He unconsciously reached for his hand sanitizer, then caught himself and put it back without using it. He took the music box Brey had given him and lifted its lid. The sweet, gentle sound of its tines rang through his office. Kier spoke softly the words of the hymn, "Then pealed the bells more loud and sweet, God is not dead nor doth he sleep. The wrong shall fail the right prevail, so peace on earth good will to men."

Forgiven. Just like that.

CHAPTER

Forty-two

There was a gentle knock on the door and Linda walked in. Kier looked up at her as he shut the lid to the music box. She sat down in one of the chairs in front of his desk.

"Nice party," he said.

"You paid for it."

"How much . . ." He stopped and held up his hand. "I don't want to know. I thought I told you to go home."

"I just had a few things I needed to finish up. What did you do to Vance?"

"Usual stuff. Broke him. Drove him to his knees. He was crying, wasn't he?"

"He asked me if you were dying."

"I get a lot of that lately."

"He told me that you're a good man."

"Yeah, now I know you're joking."

"I have a Christmas present for you." She reached inside her purse and brought out a scrolled piece of parchment tied with a red bow. She handed it to him.

"What's this?"

"Open it." He untied the bow, then unrolled the paper. A smile grew on his face as he read what she'd written. "You found her."

"It wasn't easy. I thought it was hopeless but then Mallorie over at the title company noticed a discrepancy on the foreclosure document. When Celeste purchased the home she had signed with a different last name than the one she used when she relinquished it. I guess she was still using her married name."

Kier looked back at the paper. "So she's a waitress."

"At a little diner in West Jordan. She's working tonight."

"On Christmas Eve?"

"Yes." A smile crossed Linda's face. "I have an idea. A really wonderful idea."

Kier looked at her. "Well, let's hear it."

CHAPTER

Forty-three

A Christmas Eve snowfall gently descended on the city like a final consecration of the season. The Blue Plate Grill was nearly as deserted as the streets outside, as people had already gone in for the evening's festivities. Inside the diner there were three customers: an elderly couple sharing a chocolate shake and fries, and an unkempt man in a booth sitting next to a canvas army surplus backpack with a rolled sleeping bag tied to its top.

Kier sat himself in a corner opposite the other diners. Laminated menus lay horizontal in a metal stand on the table next to the salt and pepper. He took one out; it was less than a minute before a young waitress approached his table. Her dishwater blond hair was pulled back and tied with an elastic. She wore a creamsicle-orange smock with a white collar and apron.

"Good evening."

Kier smiled. "Merry Christmas."

"Thank you. Did you get a chance to look over the menu?"

"Yes I did."

"What can I get for you?"

"Just a cup of coffee."

"Cream and sugar?"

"Just cream."

"Anything else? We have a pretty good mincemeat pie. It's fresh."

"Not a real fan of mincemeat. Looks too much like road kill."

"I'll take that as a *no* on the mincemeat."

"Do you have apple?"

She wrinkled her nose. "Yes, but honestly you'd be better off with the mincemeat. We have pumpkin. Our pumpkin's good."

"Pumpkin sounds great."

She looked at him a moment. "You look familiar. Have I waited on you before?"

"I don't think so. This is my first time at the . . ." He looked at his menu. ". . . Blue Plate Grill."

She smiled. "Maybe you just have one of those faces. I'll be right back with your coffee and pie."

She disappeared through a swinging door. Kier glanced around the diner. The elderly couple were now looking into each other's eyes and the other man had fallen asleep. The waitress returned a moment later with his order. She carried a can of Reddi-wip under her arm. "I forgot to ask if you wanted whipped cream on your pie."

"Love some. Thank you."

She sprayed a dollop of cream on the pie. "There you go. The sugar's in the canister, and here's your ticket. When you're ready I'll ring you up."

"You can do it now." Kier pulled out his wallet. He reached inside and brought out a bill. "Here, keep the change."

Celeste stared at the bill then handed it back. "You gave me a hundred."

He put his wallet back in his pocket. "I know. Merry Christmas."

She looked at him gratefully. "Thank you."

"So how'd you get so lucky to work the Christmas Eve shift?"

"Luck had nothing to do with it. I needed the money."

Kier nodded. "Tough night to work."

"You do what you've got to do."

"I like that. It's heroic."

"Yeah, I look like a hero, don't I? Super-woman."

"Not all heroes wear capes. Or silver underwear."

She smiled.

"So who watches your boy when you work late?"

Her expression changed. "How did you know I have a boy?" she asked warily. Then she turned pale. "Are you with Child Services?"

"His name is Henry, right?"

Her eyes flashed with fear. "Please, I know he's too young to stay by himself for too long. But he's very mature for his age. And I couldn't find anyone to watch him to-night."

"Relax, Celeste, would someone from Child Services tip you a hundred dollars?"

"How did you know my name?"

"I know quite a bit about you, Celeste.

We've been looking for you for almost four weeks now."

She looked positively terrified. "Are you a bill collector?"

"Not tonight." Kier took a sip of his coffee. "So, tell me, do you still believe in Santa Claus?"

"Please, whatever I've done . . ." She started to tear up. "I'm just doing the best I can."

"Celeste, I'm not a caseworker and I'm not a bill collector. You don't need to get upset."

"Then what do you want?"

"That's the right question. I would like the chance to make things right."

She looked at him blankly. "Who are you?"

Kier took a last quick sip of his coffee and stood. "I want to show you something. But you'll need to follow me to the parking lot." Kier looked past her. "That okay, Charles?"

Celeste turned toward the kitchen. She hadn't noticed that her boss, Charles, was standing near the counter watching the exchange. He smiled at her. "It's okay Celeste. I think you should go."

She looked back and forth between the two men. "What's going on?"

Kier lightly rested his hand on her shoulder. "Come with me and see." She followed Kier out to the parking lot.

"Where are we going?"

"Your car."

Celeste's car was parked beneath a lamppost; the snow had been scraped from the roof and windows. As they approached Celeste realized that her car wasn't empty. "What's this?"

Linda was parked a few spaces away; she and Mason got out of the car, holding hands as they approached Kier and Celeste. Celeste watched the whole thing confused, as if she'd unknowingly walked into a play where everyone knew their part except her.

Linda said, "You must be Celeste."

"Please, what's going on?" Celeste asked her.

Kier motioned to her car. "See for yourself."

Celeste looked apprehensively at Linda, then walked up to her car and looked inside. The back and passenger seats were filled to the ceiling with gaily wrapped packages. She looked over to Kier, then to Linda and Mason, then back to Kier.

Kier stepped up to her. "This is my friend Linda and her son, Mason."

Mason waved. "Hi."

"Linda works for me. She found you for me. We think Henry needs to believe in Santa. And so do you."

She turned and looked at him. There were tears in her eyes. "Please, tell me who you are and why you are doing this."

"You were right when you said I looked familiar. I've never been to the diner, but we have met." Kier reached into his shirt pocket, brought out a business card and handed it to her.

She looked at the card then back up at him. "I don't understand."

"Celeste, I'm the guy who talked you into buying that home you couldn't afford, then took it from you when you couldn't pay for it."

"You're . . ."

Kier nodded. "My name is James Kier. I own Kier Company. I'm here to tell you I'm sorry. And, if possible, to make amends.

"I can't give you your house back, because someone else owns it. But I have a nice little home I think you'll like. It's in a better neighborhood, with better schools, and you would have about the same amount of equity as you lost. Which means you have your life savings back."

"What if I can't afford it now? My credit score is . . ."

"Don't worry about it. I hold the note, so I've adjusted your payment to match what you're currently paying on your apartment."

"How do you know so much about me?"

"Linda's good with details. But here's the part I think you'll really like. There's a very nice mother-in-law's apartment in the basement, so you could rent it out for enough to cover your mortgage. And I think I already have a tenant for you."

Tears began to well up in Celeste's eyes. "Why are you doing all this?"

"I'm not dying," Kier said quickly.

Linda smiled.

"Celeste, there are good people in this world. People like you who struggle, but still do their best to do the right thing. Everyday heroes. You're one of them. I'd like to be one of them someday." He felt the emotion of the situation catching him and he cleared his throat. "You have my card. Come see me in the new year and I'll drive you by the house myself. In the meantime, you should go home to your son. I'm sure there's something in those boxes he'll like. Mason was a big help. He picked out everything a boy Henry's age would want."

Tears were now running down Celeste's cheeks. "I can't believe this is happening. This is an answer to prayers."

"More than you can imagine," Kier said.

Linda walked up to her still holding Mason's hand. "Merry Christmas, Celeste."

"Thank you so much," Celeste said.

"Thank Mr. Kier. He's the one who did it all."

Celeste looked at him. "May I hug you?"

"You want to hug me?"

She nodded.

"Sure."

She threw her arms around him. "Thank you, Mr. Kier."

"My name is Jim. Now, go on home. It's Christmas Eve."

She wiped her eyes. "My shift's not over."

"No," Kier said, "you're officially checked out. I worked it out with Charles."

She glanced back at the diner. Charles was standing in the doorway, his arms crossed at his chest, and a big grin covering his face. He saluted her, then walked back inside.

"Come see me soon. We'll finish the paperwork for the loan and I'll take you by the house. And be sure to bring Henry. I'd like to apologize to him as well."

"When can we move in?"

"Any time after New Year's. As soon as I'm back to work."

She looked at Kier as fresh tears fell down her cheeks. "You are the finest man I've ever met."

Kier smiled. "Go home. Your son's waiting."

Celeste hugged Kier again, then she hugged Linda and Mason and climbed into her car. She waved to them as she drove off.

Linda walked over next to Kier. "Well done, boss."

"That went well. Better, at least, than my visit with Grimes."

Linda grinned. "This has been the best Christmas. For both of us, huh, Mason?"

"Yep." He nodded vigorously.

Kier nodded. "You know, that was kind of fun."

"And you didn't need to buy Mason that remote control car," Linda gently chided.

"It was all business. Shopping consultants get paid well."

She took a few steps back and looked at him. "You did it, you know. You completed the list."

"Well, a success rate of one out of five isn't great, but you take what you can get. Which reminds me, you left a very important business associate off the list."

Linda looked concerned. "Which one?"

"You. Mason tells me he gets home from school around two-fifteen. It's good to have a mother there when you get home. The occasional baked cookies, asking how the day went, simple things, but fond memories for a child. I'm thinking we should try a little experiment. You work at the office in the morning, then at lunch you go home and work the rest of the day. I'll get you a laptop and a dedicated line for the computer. What do you think?"

"Really?"

"Of course, this will affect your salary a little."

"How little?"

"Probably about five hundred a month."

She frowned. "I appreciate you being flexible for me, Mr. Kier, but we couldn't get by on that."

"Oh." He rubbed his head. "Well, then we better make it an even thousand."

She looked at him alarmed.

"I'm giving you a *raise*, Linda."

She started to cry. "I don't know what to say."

"It's easy. Say thank you."

"Thank you."

"You're welcome. Now I've got to get home. I've kept Sara waiting too long already."

Linda suddenly leaned forward and kissed his cheek. "Celeste was right, you know. You are a good man. The finest. Merry Christmas boss. And give Sara my best."

"Merry Christmas, Linda." He looked at Mason. "And you too, big guy."

"Thank you, Mr. Kier."

Linda took Mason's hand and turned to walk away.

"Linda," he called after her.

She turned back. "Yes."

"Thank you."

A wide smile crossed her face. "You're welcome."

CHAPTER

Forty-four

Next year I'm putting up lights, Kier thought as he pulled into his driveway, then quickly thought, *No, I'll hire someone to do it*.

He parked in the driveway next to the nurse's car. As he walked in he found her in the kitchen sitting by the telephone, writing in Sara's chart.

"How is she?"

The nurse quickly looked up. From her expression he could tell that something wasn't right. "I'm glad you're here."

"What's wrong?"

"I was just going to call you. She took a turn maybe a half hour ago."

"A turn?"

"I think it's time, Mr. Kier."

Kier's chest constricted. "Where's my son?"

"He was here with his fiancée, but Sara made them go up to Juliet's parents in Ogden."

"Have you called him?"

"I tried just a minute ago, but he didn't answer."

Kier pulled out his cell phone and dialed Jimmy's number but it went right to voice mail. "Do you have a number for Juliet?"

"I might." She walked over to the refrigerator and ran her finger down a list of names and numbers. "Here it is."

Kier looked at the number and dialed. A young female voice answered. "Hello?"

"Juliet, this is James, Jimmy's father. Is Jimmy with you?"

"He's talking to my dad. Is something wrong?"

"I need to talk to him right away."

"I'll get him." He heard her say, "It's your father."

Jimmy's voice was cautious. "Hello?"

"You need to come home. Right away."

"We're on our way."

Kier turned to the nurse. "Have you heard from her sister?"

"Ms. Beth is still out of town. Would you like me to call?"

"Please."

Kier walked down the hallway to Sara's room. He could hear the quiet hiss of the oxygen apparatus. He gently opened the door and looked inside. Sara's eyes were closed. He went in and sat in the chair next to her and took her hand.

"Hey, beautiful."

She smiled at the sound of his voice though she didn't open her eyes. She said weakly, "Hi."

"Merry Christmas." He kissed her cheek.

"I didn't get you anything," she said.

"Not even coal?"

"You're not a bad boy."

"You gave me everything I wanted."

She opened her eyes and looked into his.

Kier ran the back of his hand gently over her cheek. "You never stopped believing in me, did you?"

"I never stopped loving you."

He rubbed her hand. "How are you feeling?"

She didn't answer but closed her eyes again and swallowed. Tears ran down her cheeks. Kier couldn't hold back his own.

"I'm sorry I can't stop this," she said. "I'm so sorry."

He took a tissue from the nightstand and wiped the tears from her face. "I'm just sorry I wasted all that time." They were both silent for a moment. He took her hand and gently ran his fingers down hers. "Are you afraid?"

"A little."

"Just think of all the people who will be waiting for you. It will be like a Who concert. They'll have to take tickets."

Her laugh erupted into a cough.

". . . me, on the other hand."

"I'll be waiting," she said.

"I doubt they'll let you in where I'm going."

"Remember how I used to sneak into your room without your dad knowing?"

Kier smiled in recollection. "How could I forget that?" He gently ran his finger over her lips. "With you there, it wouldn't be hell."

"Without you, it wouldn't be heaven."

He lay his head on her shoulder and she kissed the top of his head. For nearly twenty minutes they sat until the silence was broken by the doorbell. A moment later the nurse entered. She had a bemused expression on her face. "Mr. Kier?"

"Yes?" he said without looking up.

"There's a delivery . . ."

"Tell them I'll be right out."

She left.

"A delivery?" Sara asked.

"Remember what you said at your mother's funeral?"

"I said a lot of things."

"Yes. You said, 'It's a shame that people give flowers too late.' I'll be right back." He walked outside the room and a moment later he came back in carrying a large bouquet of daisies. He set them on the nightstand next to her.

"I love daisies."

"I know."

"They're beautiful."

"I'm glad you approve, because I got you a few of them." He turned toward the door and said, "Bring them in."

A man walked in with a cart of flowers; he was followed by another, then still another. Sara's smile broadened. "What did you do?"

"I think I bought up every daisy in the city. Probably the state. A thousand should be enough."

"You bought me a thousand daisies?"

"Yes."

"You're crazy." Her delighted smile belied her words.

He smiled at her. "I've been called worse."

She kept smiling as the men came and went, filling the room with flowers. "I don't think the room will hold them all."

"We'll see."

"How did you get someone to do this on Christmas Eve?"

"Money's good for some things."

"They'll be nice at my funeral."

Kier's smile fell. "Don't say that. Please."

✦

The flowers covered nearly every available surface in the room. Sara held his hand as tightly as she could.

"What do you need from me?" Kier asked.

"Take care of our boy."

"I will. I promise."

"He's a good boy."

"I know. You did a good job with him. I'll take good care of him. Not as good as you did, but I'll do my best. I'll get myself a little bracelet that says WWSD?"

"WWSD?"

"What Would Sara Do?"

She smiled. "No, please don't do that."

"I might. It's a good reminder for a lot of things." He pressed his cheek against hers. "I love you."

"I know. That's all I really wanted for Christmas."

CHAPTER

Forty-five

By ten o'clock Sara's pain had clearly grown more intense. Kier couldn't stand watching her suffer.

"The nurse will give you more medication."

"No," Sara said, "not until Jimmy gets here."

Jimmy and Juliet arrived a little before eleven. Jimmy went straight to Sara's side, his face tight with anxiety. Juliet stopped and looked around at all the flowers. "Oh my. They're beautiful."

Sara looked lovingly at her son and took

his hand. "I'm sorry I let you down, darling, I tried to make it to your wedding."

"Mom, you've never let me down." He started to cry. "You've never let me down. You've always been there for me. I love you."

"I love you, Jimmy. I need you to trust me now. I need you to promise me two things."

"Anything."

"First." She stopped, letting a wave of nausea pass. "First, give your father a chance. Open your heart to him. Promise me."

He looked at his father, then back at her. "I promise."

"Good," she said with relief. "Good. Now where is Juliet?"

Juliet was leaning against Jimmy. She stepped forward, grasping Sara's hand. "I'm here, Mom."

Sara took Juliet's hand. "Promise me that you won't delay your wedding. I will be there, you just won't see me."

Juliet looked at Jimmy, both of them in tears.

"We promise," Jimmy said.

"We promise," Juliet echoed.

Sara exhaled. "Thank you." She grimaced

with pain. Kier squeezed her hand, then went out and got the nurse. She came in carrying a bottle filled with amber liquid and placed a few drops under Sara's tongue. She checked her blood pressure then left the room. Sara's eyes closed and her face relaxed as the drug took effect. The three of them sat next to Sara, keeping a silent vigil. At midnight the grandfather clock in the home's lobby chimed. Kier said, "Merry Christmas, my love."

Sara's eyes fluttered opened. She looked around the room as if trying to remember where she was. Then she spoke softly. "Is it Christmas?"

"Yes."

Her words came slow and slurred, but still distinguishable. "We made it."

Kier struggled to control his voice. "Happy twenty-fifth anniversary."

Sara smiled. A few minutes later she fell asleep and her breathing became shallower. At 1:47 she opened her eyes, and looked up into the corner of the room. She said, "Mom."

All three of them looked to where she gazed, but saw nothing. They knew it would be soon.

Kier held her hand tightly, as if he could keep her with him by force of will. Just before she went her eyes opened once more and she looked at him. She held his hand with the last of her strength, then her grip relaxed. Kier leaned over and kissed her forehead. Then he dropped his head to her breast and wept.

CHAPTER

Forty-six

Sara Ellen Kier was pronounced dead at 2:42 A.M. Christmas morning. After the men from the mortuary had taken her body Kier sat alone in her room, his head in his hands, sobbing. Juliet walked up to him and knelt before him. "Mr. Kier, I'm Juliet. We've never met. But I'm so sorry."

Kier looked up. His eyes were puffy and red. "Thank you. Sara told me what a wonderful young woman you are. You are welcome in this family."

"Thank you, Mr. Kier."

"Please, call me Jim."

"May I call you Dad?"

"I would be honored." He closed his eyes again, overcome with emotion. Juliet put her arms around him as Jimmy watched from across the room. After a few minutes Kier looked up at his son. Jimmy was also in anguish and it broke his heart to see his son's pain. "Come here, son."

Juliet stepped back. Jimmy hesitated a moment, then remembering his promise to his mother, walked over. Then he put his arms around his father and the two of them wept for the loss of a woman they both loved.

EPILOGUE

Sara Ellen Kier, wife, mother and friend, passed away early on Christmas Day, surrounded by those she loved most. Sara was a woman of grace, love, and forgiveness. She will be dearly missed by all who knew her. She is survived by her loving husband, James, and her son, James Kier II.

Sara was buried at the Salt Lake cemetery three days after Christmas. True to their promise, four days later Jimmy and Juliet were married. Kier was part of the wedding party. At the rehearsal dinner the night before, Jimmy gave an emotional tribute to his mother, then raised a glass for a toast. "My mother was my past, for which I will always be grateful. My father is my future. To the future." Kier raised his glass, his eyes filled with tears. "To the future," he said.

✳

Kier moved back into the home he and Sara had built. He went back to his condo only once, to get his things, then sold it, with its furnishings, that February.

✦

Kier found Jimmy and Juliet's first home for them—a beautiful, newly remodeled basement apartment in the home of young single mother—Celeste Hatt.

✦

The following summer, as a birthday present, Kier took Jimmy on a long overdue father-and-son excursion—a fishing trip to Alaska. They filled their freezer with enough salmon and halibut to last several years and created memories that would last a lifetime. The day after they returned home, Kier asked Jimmy and Juliet to come by the house where Kier surprised his son with his real birthday present—a one-thousand-square-foot art studio, stocked with the best art supplies money could buy, built in the basement of Kier's home.

"I've heard that great artists need to suffer," Kier told Jimmy at the studio's unveiling, "and I can't think of any better way to accomplish that than for you to move in with me."

Jimmy laughed, then embraced his father. The truth was, the studio was Kier's

way to keep his family close. When Jimmy
spent time at the studio he and Juliet would
often stay the evening with Kier, eating dinner and visiting. Kier and Juliet became
close friends and two years later, when Juliet gave birth to a daughter, Kier became a
devoted grandfather, reserving most of his
Friday nights to watch his granddaughter,
Sara Grace.

✦

Linda took Kier up on his offer and for the
next year worked half days at home. It
proved to be a greater blessing than either
of them anticipated, as her husband, Max,
passed away just fourteen months later.
She was forever grateful for the time they
were able to spend together in those final
months. Today, Linda is James Kier's
greatest advocate and fan.

✦

Kier decided he was not satisfied with the
results of his initial contacts to the list, so a
few weeks after getting back to business,
he set out to finish what he'd begun. He
started again with Grimes, though prudently
this time, by phone. His first and second at-
tempts weren't much more productive than
his initial visit to Grimes's house (Grimes

screamed obscenities, then hung up), though less painful. Finally Kier had Lincoln send Grimes a certified letter threatening to file assault charges if he didn't appear at a meeting at Kier's office and, as an added measure, had it delivered by an off-duty police officer in uniform. Grimes arrived at the appointed time and location—angry, anxious, and outnumbered by Kier's staff, which included two burly project foremen who were there to ensure the peace.

In front of everyone, Kier formally apologized to Grimes, then made him an offer he would have been a fool to refuse. Grimes didn't. Today, Eddie Grimes manages all commercial projects for the Kier Company. On the one-year anniversary of his employment, Kier took Grimes out to lunch at his table at Rossi's. The men shared a fine meal, drinks, and laughs. Then Kier gave Grimes an unexpected gift: stock equaling 3 percent of the Kier Company. Grimes, physical by nature, hugged him. The two men have become the best of friends.

✦

With Linda's assistance, Kier tracked down Gary Rossi's wife, Melissa. She was more forgiving than Rossi's sister. Kier returned to her half ownership of the restaurant, a check for the profits due her, and created scholarship funds for each of her three children. Now, as one of Kier's business partners, Melissa and her three children attend the Kier Christmas party every year.

✦

Kier never went back to see Estelle Wyss, though he did make a donation to a charity in her name, a scholarship endowment through the University of Utah that funds an Italian study abroad program for one young woman each year.

✦

Kier never visited Carnes again. Carnes's book, *Predator or Prey*, was released nationally the following May. To Kier's dismay the book was dedicated to him; Carnes was true to his word and sent him a signed first edition copy. There was never a second edition. The next December, Kier found a signed copy of the book on sale for three dollars on the entryway bargain table of a Barnes & Noble.

✦

Two years after Sara's death, Kier turned the operation of Kier Company over to Tim Brey and left to create the Sara E. Kier

Foundation, a nonprofit organization that builds shelters for runaway youth. In so doing he finally fulfilled his dream of helping troubled youth. There are seven facilities in operation today.

✴

In one of the Thanksgiving editions of the *Salt Lake Tribune* there was an article quoting several prominent Utahns on the "true meaning of Christmas." Kier was one of those interviewed. This was Kier's response:

> The true meaning of Christmas? God's grace. And the understanding that we cannot earn grace any more than we can bargain for love. By its very nature, grace must be unearned and freely given, without cost, constraint, or commandment. The best we can do is to open our hearts to receive it wholly, with all our strength, desire, and intent, that we might become children of the Gift. Anyway, that's what I think Christmas is about. But what do I know, I'm just a carpenter.

JOIN RICHARD'S READERS CLUB

Join Richard's readers club and receive
exclusive book updates, online gifts, event
information and other great
benefits all FREE. To join go to
www.richardpaulevans.com
and click on:

JOIN RICHARD'S MAILING LIST

And welcome to the club!

Become Richard's friend on Facebook

Add Richard Paul Evans as your Facebook
friend or, to receive updated event
information, join the Richard Paul Evans
fan page. (Real fans do both!)

My Christmas List

1.

2.

3.

4.

5.

When Richard Paul Evans sat down to write *The Christmas Box,* he never imagined his book would become a number one bestseller. The quiet story of parental love and the true meaning of Christmas made history when it became simultaneously the number one hardcover and paperback book in the nation. Since then, he has written thirteen consecutive *New York Times* bestsellers. He is one of the few authors in history to have had books on both the fiction and nonfiction bestseller lists and has won several awards for his books, including the 1998 American Mothers Book Award, two first-place Storytelling World Awards, and the 2005 *Romantic Times* Best Women's Novel of the Year Award.

Four of Evans's books have been made into major television productions, starring such acclaimed actors as Maureen O'Hara, James Earl Jones, Richard Thomas, Ellen Burstyn, Naomi Watts, Vanessa Redgrave, Christopher Lloyd, and Rob Lowe.

During the spring of 1997, Evans founded the Christmas Box House International, an organization devoted to building shelters and providing services for abused and neglected children. Such shelters are operational in Moab, Vernal, Ogden, and Salt Lake City, Utah. To date more than 20,000 children have been placed in Christmas Box House facilities. In addition, his book *The Sunflower* was the motivating factor in the creation of the Sunflower Orphanage in Peru. Evans was awarded the Volunteers of America National Empathy Award and the *Washington Times* Humanitarian of the Century Award.

An acclaimed speaker, Evans has shared the podium with such notable personalities as President George W. Bush, President George H. W. and Barbara Bush, former

British Prime Minister John Major, Ron Howard, Elizabeth Dole, Deepak Chopra, Steve Allen, and Bob Hope. He has been featured on the *Today* show and *Entertainment Tonight*, as well as in *Time, Newsweek, People*, the *New York Times*, the *Washington Post, Good Housekeeping, USA Today, TV Guide, Reader's Digest*, and *Family Circle*. Evans lives in Salt Lake City, Utah, with his wife, Keri, and their five children.